LUCIFER UNEMPLOYED

Lucifer Unemployed

Aleksander Wat

Translated by Lillian Vallee

With a Foreword
by Czesław Miłosz

Northwestern University Press   Evanston, Illinois

Northwestern University Press
Evanston, Illinois 60201

Translated from the original Polish, *Bezrobotny Lucyfer,* first published
1927 by F. Hoesick, Warsaw. Published 1988 by Polonia Book Fund
Limited, London. Copyright © 1927 by Aleksander Wat, renewed by
Paulina Wat and Andrzej Wat. Northwestern University Press edition
published by arrangement with Paulina Wat and Andrzej Wat. Trans-
lation © 1990 by Northwestern University Press. All rights reserved.

"Lucifer Unemployed" appeared in slightly different form in *Artful
Dodge,* Spring 1981, Fall 1981, and Spring 1982. "Long Live Europe!"
appeared in slightly different form in *Artful Dodge,* Spring 1981.

Library of Congress Cataloging-in-Publication Data

Wat. Aleksander.
    [Bezrobotny Lucyfer. English]
    Lucifer unemployed / Aleksander Wat; translated by Lillian
Vallee.
        p.   cm
    Translation of: Bezrobotny Lucyfer.
    ISBN 0-8101-0839-9.—ISBN 0-8101-0840-2 (pbk.)
    I. Title.
PG7158.W28B413   1990
891.8'537—dc20
                                                        89-29945
                                                            CIP

To my Wife

CONTENTS

FOREWORD BY CZESŁAW MIŁOSZ

In Europe the 1920s ran their course with great avant-garde experimentation in poetry and prose. The First World War had struck at the very foundations of European tradition; but for many, including the young Polish poet Aleksander Wat, these were "happy ruins," and they grew drunk on the freedom of destroying traditional forms.

Born in Warsaw in 1900, Wat studied philosophy at the university and was a cofounder of Polish futurism. Vladimir Mayakovski, who stopped in Warsaw a few times during his travels west, called him a "born futurist," even though Wat himself rather preferred to speak of his "dadaist" beginnings. In 1920, he published a volume of poems entitled *Ja z jednej strony i Ja z drugiej strony mego mopsozelaznego piecyka* (Me from One Side and Me from the Other Side of My Pug Iron Stove).

Wat's next book, *Lucifer Unemployed* (1927), consisted of stories or, rather, paradoxical parables which, when read today, bear all the stylistic features of the period, but impress the reader nevertheless with their concentrated energy. This book was very significant to Wat's intellectual development as an act of radical distrust and scorn of civilization, which brought about his conversion to the new faith of communism.

In the years 1929-31, Wat was the very competent editor of the influential communist publication *Miesiecznik Literacki* (The Literary Monthly), which appeared in Poland in spite of censorship. After the monthly was shut down, Wat spent a few months in prison.

The outbreak of World War II in the fall of 1939 caught Wat in Warsaw, from where he escaped to the occupied Soviet zone created by the pact between Hitler and Stalin. There he was arrested and served time in various Soviet prisons, first on charges of being a Zionist, then for being a Trotskyite, and once even on suspicion of being an agent of the Vatican. Wat's direct contact with Soviet life led him to a complete revision of his views. He returned to Poland from Soviet Asia in 1946 after a protracted search to find his wife and son, who had been deported there. At the end of his tumultuous life, Wat calculated that he had known fourteen prisons.

Wat's renewed literary activity in postwar Poland soon brought charges of unorthodoxy, and he was denied the right to publish his work. The shock of returning to the familiar pattern provoked an attack of illness from which Wat never completely recovered. Nevertheless, his situation was considerably altered by the post-1956 liberalization. In 1957 he published a volume of poetry, *Wiersze* (Poems), which received a literary prize and was warmly received by the younger generation.

Because of his ill health, Wat lived abroad from 1959 in France, Italy, and the United States. In 1964-65 he lived in Berkeley, California, where, fascinated by his gift for storytelling, I tape-recorded over forty sessions with him. Wat returned to Paris, where he died in 1967. A volume of his collected poems, *Ciemne świecidło* (Dark Trinket), was published in Polish after his death in Paris, and in 1977, the memoirs I recorded, *Mój Wiek* (My Century), was published in London. (It was later published in English as *My Century: The Odyssey of a Polish Intellectual.*) This work is undoubtedly one of the most important European testaments to our epoch.

Wat's high standing in Poland as a witness and participant in historic events mirrors the growing recognition of his importance as a poet. Among his admirers, I have translated a certain number of his poems into English (*Mediterranean Poems*, 1977). A broader selection, *With the Skin*, translated in collaboration with Leonard Nathan, will be published soon.

There can be no better introduction to *Lucifer Unemployed* than Wat's own words in *My Century*:

> A very simple story. I couldn't bear nihilism, or let's say, atheism. If you go through those stories systematically, one after the other, you'll see that what I put together in *Lucifer* was a confrontation of all humanity's basic ideas—morality, religion, even love. It's especially paradoxical and interesting that just then I was going through the second year of a great love. But that cerebral questioning and discrediting of love was thorough, taken right to the end. The discrediting of the very idea of personality . . . everything in general brought into question. Nothing. Period. Finished. *Nihil.* *

According to him these stories, written in 1924 and 1925, explain how intellectuals became advocates of totalitarian movements:

> There's a short story by Graham Greene, one of his best. A man goes away from home on vacation and some young hoodlums take over his house. They take out everything in the house, they dismantle the staircases, they remove everything; only the walls are left. Later, the man comes back, sees his house from a distance. Everything looks entirely normal, the way it was before. But he finds the interior consumed, an empty space. And my malice of that time, that terrible obstinate malice, came from a sort of intellectual hoodlumism. From a feeling that though the outward forms had been preserved, inside everything had been eroded, removed, cleaned out. It turned out that this was more than I could bear. I closed my eyes to it. I locked up all

---

*Aleksander Wat, *My Century: The Odyssey of a Polish Intellectual*, ed. and trans. Richard Lourie (Berkeley: Univ. of California Press, 1987), p. 20.

my ideas, everything, I threw the key into the abyss, the sea, the Vistula, and threw myself into the only faith that existed then.

There was only one alternative, only one global answer to negation. The entire illness stemmed from that need, that hunger for something all-embracing. In fact, communism arose to satisfy certain hungers. The phenomenon was inevitable insofar as powerful hungers had arisen in modern societies, even in those of the nineteenth century. One of those hungers was the hunger for a catechism, a simple catechism. That sort of hunger burns in refined intellectuals much more than it does in the man on the street.*

Wat did not live to see the collapse of dogmas considered untouchable in his day and will not see the edition of his writings currently being prepared for publication in Warsaw. I do not know how he would have reacted to the idea of presenting *Lucifer Unemployed* to American readers. I think that as a man sorely tried by history he would have been glad to know that his youthful anticipations grasped something of the sinister dynamic peculiar to our own time, when our planet is becoming a global village. Fortunately for him, Wat was not just a despairing moralist. Just as in his zany poems where he clowns around, turns cartwheels, and sticks out his tongue, there is a lot of film comedy—perhaps even the Marx Brothers—in *Lucifer Unemployed*.

_____

*Ibid.

THE ETERNALLY WANDERING JEW

1

"Hello! Hello! This is New York speaking. A pound 3.20. In the morning I leave by dirigible R 5. See you at five in London."

The telephone was disconnected. The hand of Baron Gould rested motionless on the support of the armchair. The hand of a croupier, raking in gold from the gambling table of Europe. A hand with swollen veins—a railway junction, obscured by strands of cigarette smoke—with five wide fingers, wide tracks to five capitals, to five parts of the world. Now the tracks rested on the carved wood of the arm.

The July evening lay on the terrace of the seventeenth story of the Hotel Livingston—an exhausted barbarian in fetters of luxury. Baron Gould daydreamed; he listened to the din of the city and remembered his childhood. The oval of the murky Galician town, the silver candlesticks spattered with melted wax, Friday evening, the hands, wrinkled and yellowed like Palestine, of the old woman in the green velvet dress embroidered with silver, her blessing, and the apple and orange wrapped in a handkerchief for her grandson fluttered over the sclerotic pounding heart of New York with a speed greater than three hundred thousand kilometers per second.

The baron remembered his childhood and listened to the tumult of the city; he was hard and taut with daydreams. The swish of trams, the scattering echoes of church bells, bustling crowds, groans of jolted concrete and the indistinct musical undercurrent of the city, which rhythmically moves the beautifully healthy thighs of women wearing little chapels of sex under the chasubles of their dresses and strains the muscles of the policeman who keeps the streets tethered. Sweet, intoxicating sound! It is possible that farther down, perhaps just a hundred feet away, another orchestra was striking up, a tempest of transmissions, clatter of steel, menacing roar of factory halls, saturating the ear of the proletariat with the delicious hymn of revenge—but here the sound was soft and coarse, wild and virginal, sweet as a kiss in the rain, wavy as permed hair, more rollicking than a jazz band. Baron Gould heard still another sound: a voice rushing down the trumpet of the street, shouting Baltazar's words: TIME IS MONEY. It was time shouting: let's get going! Down there they knew this—they hurried. Time is the enemy, thought the baron. He felt he was aging. Time deducted more and more from his store of dreams—the energizing battery for people of action. Time was diminishing his chances; time, that cruel athlete, had knocked flat the obese body of the banker. Time was his enemy, money his friend. Baron Gould belonged to a race that the enchanted bird of money often rescued from the pyres of martyrdom and the jaws of annihilation. Money is a paradox. And that is why this paradoxical race took such a liking to it. Money is the algebra in the arithmetic of things. That is why this people possessed it—the algebra of peoples. Baron Gould was a convert but a loyal son of his people. He accumulated money—abstract and material, individualistic and impersonal paradoxes—but he desired something else, for he was the son of a people that gave its life for money and its money for the Bible. Baron Gould desired greatness as people had once desired their soul's salvation. He desired to rule time as he ruled space, by skewering Paris, London, New York, Yokohama, Sydney, and Vienna onto the awl of his business dealings. He was the son of a people who were witnesses and cocreators of history. He desired to stop history, turn it back and wrap it around himself. He desired to change the impersonal power of a banker into the personal sway of a reformer. In the meantime, he subsidized missions, convents, sects, Tibetan monasteries, Bet Ha-Midrashim. He had a son who was a cleric in Rome and he himself attended the synagogue on the Day of Atonement and prayed and fasted. He yearned for greatness as people had once longed for martyrdom. Time was his enemy. It made him richer in gold but more deficient in greatness. Enormous columns of figures, skyscraping towers of figures grew—Paris, London, New York, Berlin, Vienna, Sydney—but the baron desired something else: he desired greatness. Even if it became the hand of fury, erasing towers of figures from the face of the earth?

One evening a red-haired youth announced himself to the baron and, practically with tears in his eyes, begged the baron to finance a worldwide communist revolution. He presented a plan that guaranteed flawless success. Weighing the plan in his hand, Baron Gould felt how light the security of Europe was. He had also read a few books about communism. The same figures, organized in different columns. He desired something else: he desired greatness. For several evenings in a row he discussed dogma and the revolution, the meaning of life and all the cosmic issues with the red-haired youth, and in the end he set him up in a well-paying position with one of his London offices.

Now, one July evening on the terrace of the seventeenth story of the Hotel Livingston, Baron Gould is dreaming of a great historical deed, he is listening to the hum of the city and remembering his childhood. Into the sweet and brutal sounds, into the sounds soft and undulating as waved hair, time thrusts its sharp dissonances. Baron Gould recalls Holbein's engravings: a young woman listening to the violin of death. Baron Gould (the Stradivarius of the stockmarket) was all of them, the violin, the young woman and death that July evening when Nathan, a Talmudist from Zebrzydowo, asked him: So now what?

2

There is always mud in Zebrzydowo. In the spring it runs in wavy streams; in the summer it is thick, deep, and black; in the fall it is sticky and gummy; and in the winter it crunches underfoot. In Zebrzydowo there is an old yeshiva. Marks left by Chmielnicki's bullets are still visible on its pockmarked walls. Nothing has changed since that time: centuries pass by hospitably, quietly, lazily, as if they had taken a liking to splashing around in the mud of Zebrzydowo. Only the most recent century—the wicked plunderer slithers up with false steps and always manages to abduct another victim: yesterday one, today another, tomorrow a third will cut his robe short, cover his head with haberdashery worn by pallbearers and Christians, shave his beard and sidelocks, as if the robe, skullcap, and sidelocks were not the adornments of a Jew.

The director of the yeshiva is Reb Mordecai; the brightest pupil is Nathan, an orphan, who lost his parents in a pogrom. When he was eight years old, he recited a hundred pages from the Gemara by heart. At fifteen, he was known for his wisdom and extraordinary memory. He read in books that were bound in brown leather, embossed with gold, and had torn bindings, and only rarely would he look up at the tome written in God's undecipherable hand. At those moments he prayed fervently, full of awe and amazement at the Eternal One.

One evening, after leaving the synagogue, he noticed a distant figure that reminded him of the Rebbe. And because he needed his advice regarding an intricate point in the Talmud, he called out: "Rebbe! Rebbe! Rebbe!" When the supposed rebbe turned around, Nathan was horrified to discover he had made a mistake: instead of the jaundiced, freckled face of the rebbe, he was looking at the rosy, round, towheaded, blue-eyed face of the parish priest. (A trifling event which impressed itself deeply upon Nathan's soul. He recalled it many years later as the prophetic annunciation of his later deeds.)

In his nineteenth year, Nathan knew more than all the Talmudists in Zebrzydowo. Reb Mordecai was deeply concerned. In former days, he wouldn't have had to worry. Nathan would have grown in his wisdom in the home of his wealthy father-in-law. That is why a Jew plies his trade, wheels and deals, and cheats six days a week: so his son or son-in-law can sit at home over the Talmud, so that his house can glow with the light of that jewel of Israel. But today everything has changed for the worse.

Nathan's future appears uncertain—Reb Mordecai suffered profound anguish over this.

The day before leaving the yeshiva, Nathan found out that he had been living and studying—as had his friends—at the expense of a well-known benefactor, a powerful Jew, the friend and lender to kings, Baron Gould, who lived abroad in Vienna. From then on Nathan could think of nothing else. All of his affection, all the fervor of his orphan's dreams were transferred to the distant guardian. He felt that the bond joining him to the baron could not, should not be broken now just when he had discovered it. In his imagination Nathan arrayed the baron in all that was picturesque. He knew that Baron Gould was mightier than kings. He had seen them on the cards they used in Hanukkah games and he admired their splendor. Baron Gould's splendor, therefore, must be even greater. From that moment on, he desired but one thing: to see him. Nathan dreamed of him, he made him responsible for the direction of his life, and he demanded further guidance. He grew close to his idealized image, he felt him to be the highest reality, he took into consideration the views he imagined the Baron held, he gave in to him and rebelled. He became wild, alien, locked in himself; he spoke to no one. People shook their heads and said that his great learning had cast him into melancholy. Until one day he rolled his tallith, phylacteries, a loaf of bread, and a few books into a bundle and, asking the way to Vienna, left Zebrzydowo.

When he left the town, the striped sky looked like a tallith and the sun, slashed by the horizon, like phylacteries. In two months he made it to Warsaw. In three, he reached Vienna. Patience is a characteristic of his people. Patience led his people out of Egypt and patience returned them to the promised land after several thousand years. A Jew stands before a wall and waits until the wall lets him through. There were many walls on Nathan's way. Some the Almighty changed into bridges, others stepped out of the way by themselves. In Vienna, Nathan found out that the baron had left for Paris. So he inquired where Paris was and set out. Everywhere he met sons of his people. He knew that the world was flat and enormous, but the sons of his people whom he met shortened the distance, bringing Zebrzydowo closer. In three months, he arrived in Paris. He looked at the vastness, splendor, and strangeness of this city, but nothing surprised him. He knew all this from descriptions in the Bible, from the prophets and the Talmud. Formerly it had been called Sodom and Gomorrah, Babylon, Rome. Today it was called Warsaw, Vienna, Paris. Only the names had changed, the sin had remained. One dies, another is born, and this is how it will be until the coming of the Messiah, who will come on a white mule from the East. Miraculous machines, enormous edifices, godless people, luxury and debauchery—he had read about them earlier, he knew them in detail while still in the yeshiva and he remained indifferent. For everywhere, in every wafer of sin beat but one heart—that of the holy Torah. He found it in every city. It beat in the sinful body of cities. He walked away from it, yet it was always close by. He grew distant from it, yet he did not leave it behind. He walked endlessly yet always came upon the center of the earth. Paris gaped in amazement at this young, exotically dressed Jew—who often stopped in the boulevards in the evening, on the place Blanche or the rue de la Paix, in the middle of the sidewalk with his face turned toward the east, and prayed, whispering incomprehensible Hebrew prayers. People wrote about him in magazines and published his picture— Nathan paid no attention at all to this, he thought only of the baron.

But the baron was no longer in Paris; he was now in New York. Nathan inquired where New York was and set out. In Calais he saw the sea. He was disappointed. He knew of course that it was enormous, yet here he saw an expanse that was limited by the line of the horizon, just as stretches of land were. It took Nathan over a year to get to New York. The baron lived at the Hotel Livingston. Nathan did not know what he would say to him. He did not think about that. He wished only to see him. On the terrace of the seventeenth story of the hotel he finally saw Baron Gould. Only now, after two years of wandering from Zebrzydowo to New York, was Nathan truly astonished for the first time. He had become fond of an image of the Baron that was more colorful and splendid than the pictures of kings on playing cards and now before him was a man that looked exactly like everyone else. At this hour in Zebrzydowo it was Saturday afternoon. The Jews were returning from the synagogues, each in a tallith; the children splashed in the mud—how pleasant to splash around in the Zebrzydowo mud! On the high terrace of the New York hotel, Nathan asked Baron Gould: So now what?

3

A few years after the war in Europe incidents of cannibalism were multiplying. In Russia, on the wide Caspian expanses; in the West, Haarman, Denke and many other unknowns. The cannibal of Europe gasped with horror at his own face. There was talk of the need for peace, talk about the dollar, about armaments, the trial in Dayton, the crisis of democracy, the insurrection in China, the blues, the League of Nations, boxing, the new poetry, the danger of foreign races, the crisis, our endangered civilization, the conflict in Mosul, the Jews, the stock market. In Warsaw, Melbourne, Vienna, Tokyo, Berlin, Shanghai, New York, and London crashes, bankruptcies, and fires proliferated; the stock exchanges gave signs of panic, currencies rose and fell like targets at a shooting range and ran like paranoids overcome by their own anxiety. Banks crashed, bordellos flourished. Only Baron Gould grew more and more wealthy. His trusts, his counting houses raked in gold from all over the world. Nathan studied political economy at the university, greedily gulping the strange, enormous, and sophisticated culture of the West. By turn, he zealously adored Christ and then succumbed to the dialectics of Lenin. In a fever of cognition, he threw himself into the sources of all intellectual currents, always on the lookout for ever-newer ones.

In 1935, Europe was talking about the need for peace, about the perils of other races, about the upcoming war, crime, dances, anarchists, sports, America, the economic crisis, political accords, the new poetry, armaments, the end of the world, religious sects, the crisis of democracy, and Jews. In cafés the apostles advertising the destruction of civilization proselytized like tenth-century hermits, threatening everyone with Judgment Day. The gods drowned in Russian rivers years ago returned preceded by the fanfare of sectarians. Europe swayed on its clay feet. The zoological garden of Great Britain, as large as the zodiac, shattered the bars of centuries of reasons of State. Politicians were helpless in the face of the colonial beasts they had unloosed. The bourgeoisie gathered its forces and defended itself with a heroism never before known in history. Here and there it died Herostrates' death; here and there, it was utterly pauperized; in vain did it sigh after communism. The proletariat was vanishing in the vortex of the general chaos. Religiosity, sectarianism, and metaphysics penetrated through the cracked hull of the sinking ship of the world. There was talk of signs that would precede the final day. In Paris, a fifty-five-year-old newspaper vendor who had never known a man gave birth to a son with radiating skin. In London, bloody swords and riders on red horses were seen in the sky in the evenings. In Berlin, the owner of a fashion house pronounced herself the savior of the world. World finance underwent the sharp crisis of an undiagnosed illness, an illness whose bacillus eluded the efforts of the economists. On the back of the world, in Vienna, festered the largest boil: Baron Gould, dictator of the world stockmarket. Europe begged him to save her. Europe—cannibalistic, impoverished, mystical, sadistic, prostituted. But the Baron had become old and he turned a deaf ear to her pleas. Nathan was his secretary. Nathan now managed the Baron's business in New York and he wanted to distinguish himself. Fascism taught him that political upheaval was a matter of enlisting the greatest amount of idle ambitions. He turned his gaze to the East, to Zebrzydowo—ten kilometers from the nearest train station—spattered with mud. His roots were planted firmly in the old yeshiva, but the dialectics of European civilization now lodged in his head. I will be the Ark of the Covenant between the Jews and Europe, between the West and the East, daydreamed Nathan.

Baron Gould felt that this time he had to come up with something great, otherwise he would be wiped out by the avalanche of impending chaos. The moment of greatness had arrived, but of what sort of greatness? It was then that Nathan sent him a voluminous letter from New York. This is Nathan's letter:

Do not think that everything here in New York is as it was. The European bacillus has arrived on Long Island along with groups of Jewish emigrants, volumes of French poetry, and packages of hard currency. How far we have strayed from the American Ideal: each Yankee with a pipe in his mouth standing in the shadow of his own skyscraper! Unfortunately, this is all a thing of the past. Our billionaires are buying plantations in Haiti and fleeing there with their families. Bombers and arsonists, anarchists and sectarians, Ku Klux Klansmen have overrun our cities. Don't expect us to rescue you. America is no longer America! It is surrounding itself with a cordon of isolation to prepare for battle with an internal bacillus while it still has time.

We have stepped into the Middle Ages of industrialization. Our urban civilization will reach God not via a path, but via rail, wide rail, blazed by the greatest heresiarch: science. Religiosity is bearing down on us from all sides in disarray and chaos. Nevertheless I do not understand and I feel repelled by those religionists, collectors of religious instinct, crazed aesthetes, seekers of peculiarities and decorativeness, who draw their religiosity, seek salvation and false aesthetic revelations in the old editions of the church fathers, in the incunabula, in the parchment-bound folios of Saint Thomas, in the barren metaphysicians of bygone centuries, instead of sitting down to an ordinary physics textbook which contains more religious revelations than all the used bookstores of the world. It is physics that points the way of the new religion, reborn Catholicism, a religion which will, simultaneously, be a rational construction of societies. Pay close attention to what I am saying. Just as the principles of physics (on which it is based) are conventions, almost articles of faith having no proof of existence other than the fact that the laws and effects resulting from them are roughly in keeping with the experiences of the senses, so, too, the dogmas of religion (think about this), its postulates do not require any other proof of existence, except that the laws and consequences resulting from them will be roughly in keeping with the ethical and religious experience of the human soul. In this way, for example, the existence of God, which is impossible to prove, is the equivalent of the impossible-to-prove hypothesis that all of creation is subject to the same basic laws of physics, a hypothesis without which science would be impossible. There is no reason to believe that there is a contradiction between religion and physics (I include all sciences based on empirical experience under this name), using different methods and maintaining the distinctness of their areas. They share *in abstracto* the object of the experience, which in reality is often indivisible. Human society is exactly such an indivisible object, falling under both systems. The ideal social order, therefore, will be one that reconciles and coordinates these two systems: the rational system of the scientific construction of society (communism), which by itself disintegrates against the irrational atom of the soul, and the system of the religious construction of society (Catholicism)—based on dogmas of the soul's experiences—which disintegrated in contact with physics. And so neo-Catholic Marxism or Catholicism, that is, communist theocracy—*in hoc signo vinces.* But the Roman Church is dispirited and ailing, who will restore its powers? I will answer that question, too: the Jews! Let us gaze at the vast expanse of history, let us join our point of departure to Moses' burning bush, to Calvary, to Marx. What a gigantic and bright historical panorama! We see two mighty rivers, surging from the primeval stream of the nomadic tribe of Canaan, from their primal and naive unity. We see how after cutting through the entire world, eroding cliffs, piling mountains, they join again, enriched and beneficent; they return to a common riverbed, as if making up the continuation of the primal stream of Judaism, from which they flowed. Now you know why the Jews carried their Torah out of conflagration and defeat, weariness, old age, disease, and repression, why they maintained their separateness: to rediscover and rekindle it in a universal rebirth. Now you understand the secret of the Wandering Jew.

I will be more specific: only Jews have been called to create the new universal religion, to reconcile all the contradictions. They alone can create a communist theocracy. They alone have been able to hang on, like Noah, in the dregs of anarchy. Religious and godless, revolutionary and conservative, they alone are predestined to renew the world in a dictatorship based on a transcendental dogma.

Therefore, the Jews must, first of all, accept Catholicism en masse. Impossible? I would answer—*certum quia impossibile*. The time has come for us to revise our attitude toward Christianity. How many young Jews have I seen, burning with adoration for the Savior, striking their foreheads against cold church marble! How many of them have I seen feverish from a strange concoction of Zionism, Catholicism, and Communism. Millions of eastern Jews shake off the cadaverous incomprehensibility of rabbinity in mysticism, that mutation of souls. The Kabbalah has prepared them for the unity of the Trinity. Their *amor dei intellectualis* allows them to recognize themselves in the world church of the fisherman Simon Peter, in the church of John, whose logos is the logos of the Alexandrian Jew Philo. Let us not deceive ourselves: Christ has long ceased being the difference between us. The

Eternally Wandering Jew wants to rest. He will find death under the cross, death, followed by a rebirth. Two thousand years ago, the Jew denied Christ in order to exist. Today, in order to exist, he must adore him.

I will recapitulate. Jews should become the hierarchy of the Catholic clergy and rebuild the world into a new theocracy. The reforms introduced by the Vatican not long ago—unification with the Eastern church, and the accompanying abolition of celibacy—have eliminated the most important obstacle in the execution of my plan. Your money will accomplish what dialectics were unable to get done. Now is the moment to use it, otherwise . . . I dream how one autumn, when the leaves on the trees in Zebrzydowo roll up like half-yellow, wine-stained pages of the old Haggadah, how in one such autumn the venerable yeshiva of my hometown and together with it all the other yeshivas change into seminaries educating the Catholic dictators of the world. In this alone do I see its salvation.

Nathan ended the letter by saying he would arrive shortly with a well-thought-out plan of action.

4

Ten years later more and more clerics with long hawklike noses and eyes dimmed with a cosmic melancholy were evident in Rome. In the year 1965 Baron Gould's former secretary, Nathan, the Talmudist from Zebrzydowo, was elected Pope Urban IX. That year marks the beginning of a new era in the history of mankind. Pope Urban IX mobilized Europe to a holy war with invading Asia. Enormous Chinese hordes, organized by apologists of Asia, Germans, and Russian Communists, set out to conquer the world, destroying everything in its path. The Mongol onslaught was stopped at Poland's eastern border. The decisive battle was fought close to Zebrzydowo. Pope Urban IX himself stood at the head of his armies. After a prolonged battle, he defeated the Chinese, who retreated, leaving hundreds of thousands dead and wounded. Europe was saved. Europe experienced an exaltation unknown until that day. The pope was the dictator of the world. Economic reforms fused the broken backbone of Europe. Societies impoverished by the war and long unaccustomed to luxury returned to simplicity, to the communal administration of monasteries. In the year 1985 Baron Gould was canonized. In the first half of the twenty-second century there wasn't a single cleric of Aryan descent. Earlier Pope John XXIV had forbidden the clerics to intermarry with the laity. Thanks to this Jews were able to maintain their racial purity. A universal, uninterrupted peace reigned. Nothing threatened the new system of the world. The East, after its defeat on the borders of Poland, again plunged into lethargy for several centuries. The light of the Vatican fell on an America just awakening from the most terrible nihilism and destruction. Africa supplied the church with its most faithful sons. The papal armies were made up of powerful, enormous warriors from Senegal, burning with an overflowing love of Christ. The Papacy was a universal state, the largest in the history of the world.

5

Not counting the fleeting and quickly fading heresies, the new system of the world had just one dangerous enemy: anti-Semitism. Anti-Semites preferred giving up their Catholicism to making peace with the Jews. Anti-Semitism, even though it had lost its reason for being, endured by dint of its historical inertia. It attracted to itself all the malcontents, all the atheistic and anti-Catholic elements. They organized themselves, undermining the authority of the church, destroying its unity, hatching plots and creating a real threat to the omnipotence of the papacy. They occupied themselves with science, trade, and travel, amassing riches and paving the way for the rebirth of capitalism. A period of persecution soon followed. In the year 2270, Pope Pius XV issued a bull, the first in a series of orders directed against the anti-Semites/anti-Catholics. In time, they were segregated from Catholic society, they were forbidden to hold office, deprived of civil rights, confined to special areas; separate taxes were levied on them, and they were set apart with specific clothing. At the beginning of the twenty-fourth century, John Ford, descendant of an old family line that passed its anti-Semitism from father to son, became leader of the anti-Semites. He united the scattered and conspiring villages, introduced discipline and began a battle for their rights, for the freedom of his comrades. While collecting materials for an anti-clerical biography of Pope Urban IX (the former Talmudist from Poland), he traveled to Zebrzydowo. There was mud in Zebrzydowo. In the old yeshiva lived Abraham the Jew, perhaps the only one in the whole world who still practiced the Mosaic religion. Unfortunately he was the last descendant of a family which in that vast Christian world had preserved the religion of his ancestors. His father, not wanting the family to end with him, conceived Abraham of his own sister, but the Almighty had denied sex to Abraham. He obviously desired Jewry to vanish from the face of the earth. Unfathomed are his judgments.

John Ford found old brittle books in the yeshiva. Abraham taught him Hebrew and Aramaic. He initiated him into the wisdom of the old culture, to which he was the last remaining key, its last guardian on earth. The lofty wisdom of the Mishnah unveiled itself to John, the sharp dialectics of the Gemara, the stellar mysticism of the cabala. The scroll of Torah unrolled into the heavens, starred with God's scriptures.

In a history of medieval Jews, John Ford found a precise description of the persecutions his brothers were enduring. He was moved and overwhelmed by the historical analogies. In Mosaic Law, John found the lofty, severe, abstract religion of real life, as opposed to the idealism of Christianity, which, desiring to base itself on the extreme values of absolute good and absolute evil, actually indulged the torpidity of human nature. In this religion of sober reality, John Ford saw the much-desired and much-needed cult sought by his brothers, a cult which would crown their separateness, fill the void and veil it with the banner of eternity.

In the year 2320 the anti-Semites/anti-Catholics, with John Ford at their head, converted to Judaism. They began to search for old buried tomes, to build synagogues, found schools, and restore Hebrew customs and faith.

The disturbed Vatican answered them with a revival of the Holy Inquisition. In the year 2362 Pope Sextus XV named his confessor, a monk with the heart of a dove, a fanatic of the faith, the Grand Inquisitor. He was the first to make stakes flare up again in Spain, France, Italy, and Germany. The estates of the orthodox anti-Semites were confiscated, their books burned, and they themselves were sent to the stake. In the year 2380, in Spain alone, two thousand orthodox anti-Semites perished.

Thus the persecutor became the persecuted and the persecuted the persecutor.

Thus in the name of Christ did Israel avenge itself on its enemies.

6

The twenty-fifth century passed, the last century of the lay power of the papacy. The stagnation of its insular dogmatism, the disintegration and fall of the clergy, the revolutionary and critical currents of a reawakening Europe, the emancipation of science, the development of capitalism, the rebirth of lay civilization from the fifteenth to twentieth centuries began a new historical period. Catholicism ceased to play a historical role. Tempests swept over old Europe, the dawn of freedom broke over the horizon. Anti-Semite old believers slowly regained their civil rights and awakened from the horrible slumber of the ghetto, into which they had been plunged by centuries of defeat.

In the year 2900 there was mud in Zebrzydowo, the ancient, immortal mud of Zebrzydowo. In the old yeshiva, still recalling Chmielnicki's bullets, the most capable student was Nathan, an orphan who had lost his parents in a pogrom. One evening after leaving the synagogue, Nathan noticed a figure that reminded him of the rabbi in the distance. Because he needed his advice on an intricate point in the Talmud, he ran after him calling: "Rebbe! Rebbe!" When the so-called rabbi turned around, Nathan was horrified to see his mistake: instead of the antici- pated towheaded, blue-eyed face of the rabbi, the jaundiced, freckled face of the parish priest stared back at him with its hook nose and eyes veiled with a cosmic melancholy.

――――――――

Kings in Exile

1

The first mate of the English ship *Cromwell* peered at the horizon, ragged as an envelope ripped open by an impatient hand, at the dry landscape of the Arkhangel'sk coast, at the fisherwoman nursing her baby under her striped fustian, at the sky—that great mirror, where from under the fustian of clouds and fog emerged the milky breast of the sun.

Fog, he thought, and turned around, hearing steps behind him. Two natives walked onto the deck: an old man with a long gray beard dressed in a bourgeois frock coat, fatigue cap, and tree-bark moccasins, and a short, frail young man, barefoot, in a red tunic, with a thick rope around his waist. The first mate couldn't stand barbarians. He looked with equal contempt upon the smelly, dirty, slant-eyed Melanesians with curly hair and decorations of shells and straws who swarmed the eastern shores of the Pacific, and the light-eyed, blond Slavs from the White Sea. How astonished he was, therefore, when the gray-bearded newcomer spoke to him with the purest London accent: "I would like to speak with the captain."

A few hours later the *Cromwell* was sailing on the open seas. And in the evening the telegraph machines clattered from Vologda to Arkhangel'sk and from Arkhangel'sk to Moscow, to the Red fleet. A thick fog facilitated the escape of the English ship. It eluded the wandering tentacle-spotlights of the cruisers and torpedo ships propelled by the rhythmic effort of the steel muscles of the machines and the twisted muscles of the proletariat of the sea. After five weeks of sailing the *Cromwell* was hauled into the Thames at night. But only two people left the ship that night: the graybearded old man and the frail youth from Arkhangel'sk, both dressed as officers of the English Navy. On the boulevard a large mud-spattered taxi with drawn windows awaited them. Inside sat the director of the London Police. He was so tall that to bow he had to fold himself in half. "Your Majesty," he lisped in a voice full of homage.

2

Thomas Clark was a pillar of the Chicago *Tribune*. He had an unsurpassed nose for sniffing out what was happening, a splendid gift for anticipating the course of events, and the skill to integrate his daily experiences into fascinating short paragraphs, serving them up to the citizen with his morning coffee in the form of a simplified image of the world that stimulated digestion—in other words, all the qualities that make a model journalist. During the war he was tossed from one front to another, he flew over enemy countries as if he were spat from the jaws of the fronts and astride cannonballs, like Baron von Münchhausen. On the shores of the Aduga he shouted "Avanti!" along with swarthy Italians; on the banks of the Marne he offered cigars to the brave *voyous*. He retreated from the Carpathian mountains with Russian muzhiks; valiantly served the allies, the Hapsburgs, and the bankers from Wall Street; tore through Siberia to the Pacific Ocean along with the Czechs, fought in Kolchak's ranks, transported valuable documents to the English in Baku, was taken prisoner by the Bolsheviks, was imprisoned by the Cheka, escaped to Mongolia, spoke with Chutuchta in Urga, after which, sated with adventure, he returned home.

His philosophy of history was amazingly simple. He knew that a watermark showed through the pages of history: Cleopatra's nose and Newton's apple. ("If Cleopatra's nose had been a millimeter longer, the history of the world would have taken a different turn." "Newton was sitting under an apple tree one evening, meditating, when all of a sudden a falling apple revealed the law of gravity to him.") Thomas Clark knew all too well the importance of the minute detail and the role of chance. Chance governed the fate of Balkanized Europe. The firing of a telephone operator, who had diverted the pay of a girlfriend (who had broken solidarity) into the union till, unleashed a social revolution in Bulgaria. Thomas Clark was alert to the significance of facts: hence his ease in jumping from one trampoline of opinion to another and his skill at reading historical upheavals from insignificant events, qualities that made him the augur and Madame de Thebes of journalism.

3

Another of Thomas's strengths was an intimate acquaintance with Europe. He knew its cities and nationalities, markets and churches, its politicians, jazz bands, monarchs, criminals, restaurants, scholars, prisons, church hierarchy, revolutionaries, brothels (he was the anonymous author of a deluxe edition of a catalog of bordellos in postwar Europe intended for the use of American millionaires), its ministers, adventurers, inventors, journalists, fashion designers, industrialists, dancers, poets, financiers, aristocrats, spies, theaters, and doctors. He knew all the luminaries of his day and collected their photographs in albums, similar to those containing pictures of wanted criminals.

Yet only his closest friends knew the real reason for his drive. Only they knew that an especially pathological passion—the completely unbridled desire to possess women of all nations and tribes—had made Thomas an indefatigable Ahasuerus of the press. When he was thirty-five, Thomas could boast of intimate ties with almost a hundred tribes. His political pessimism derived from a limited number of ethnic groups. In order to possess the stinking female dwarf of a Pygmy tribe or the enormous Matabele gardener, he did not hesitate to travel to the Kaffirs. He arrived in England in pursuit of the last red-skinned woman of the Sioux-Oglala tribe appearing in a London music hall, and here he got wind of the secret of the *Cromwell.*

4

A few days later the Chicago *Tribune, Times, Temps,* and *Corriere della Serra* simultaneously published the extraordinary supplements. The commotion spread by newsboys screaming: Czar Nicholas II lives! The Secret of the *Cromwell!* Such was the overture to the monarchic opera buffa which constitutes the plot of our story.

5

News of the survival of Nicholas II, the heir to Alexander's throne, evoked an eruption of monarchic activity, fortified the impetus of the dreams and hopes of bankrupt courtiers, Junkers, students, *rentiers,* restorationists and panderers. In all the countries of Europe, aristocratic counterfeiters, assuming that only monarchs had the right to coin money and following the brilliant example set by the Prince Windischgrätz, started to compete with the mints of republican states, often surpassing them in precision of execution. In Italy, Mussolini recognized the moment as one appropriate to proclaiming the Holy Roman Empire. In Poland the blue generals, landholders, clergy, student fraternities and guild masters dragged out and dusted off lithographic portraits of the czar's family and felt a rising tide of nostalgia for savings account books, gold braid, samovars, the czarist police and kopecks, the sunshine of bygone days. Wilhelm II published a letter threatening to unleash civil war in Germany in the name of saving civilization, authority, and religion. Entire anthills of German kinglings and princes and Russian exiles dusted off their uniforms, decorations, and banners. The former Persian shah organized an army of marauders, Parisian pimps, and slender sutlers from la place Pigalle. The information about the survival of the czar was the fuse that ignited the musty dynamite of monarchic sentiment.

6

Thomas Clark trotted back and forth between Paris, Berlin, Budapest, Doorn, and Rome, devising and hatching a great plan under the rallying cry: "Monarchs of the World Unite!" His small cat eyes bereft of a steady point—when he looked at an object, he seemed to strip it of color and shape—ran over the agitated landscapes of an agitated continent from the air, or from the windows of speeding limousines or lightning-swift trains. During the day he was oppressed by the revolting alienness of their masks—Thomas hated nature and knew it best because he knew it from the windows of a train car. (It was with amazement that he discovered the possibility of something that was not urban civilization. Through the windows of a speeding train he was able to see for himself the enormous expanses of nature, of which cities are but a tiny, insignificant fraction. Each time he observed with involuntary amazement that trees are not houses crawling with people, that, in fact, man does not have to be a part of the tormenting, bothersome, disintegrating process of a collectivity.)

7

A Congress of dethroned monarchs convened in Geneva in December 192-. . .

The list of participants would fill a hefty volume of the Gotha Almanac.* Let us add the dethroned Turkish sultan, the Chinese

*A yearbook of European aristocracy and dynastic genealogy.— ED.

bodhi khan, the Persian shah, the Abyssinian negus and their courts. In Geneva, there was a plague of aristocrats, cinema operators, diplomats, cocaine sellers, discharged generals, correspondents, women—every inch of whose bodies was loved into discoloration—swindlers, traveling salesmen, Negroes, American girls, and an enormous number of secret agents mobilized from around the entire world. The creased pants and faces of Englishmen; the scarred and ruddy faces of Germans; the full feminine shapes of the Italians, Romanians, Brazilians, with hair that gleamed like ads for shoe polish; Yankees on wide rubber soles, with Rolls-Royces in their heads and skyscrapers in their vest pockets; slithering Russians; the lace of titles woven for centuries, the chasubles of clerics, stars, decorations, and the zodiacs of heraldic shields.

At five o'clock in the evening in the hotels of Geneva the Bourbons, Hohenzollerns, Hapsburgs, Romanovs, and Zamojskis danced the Charleston with the daughters of watchmakers, Swiss hotelkeepers, kings of grease, crude, and preserves from Dolarika.

Thomas Clark moved around in this throng and looked with pride at his work. He was let in on all the backstage secrets, he reconciled the feuding, was a go-between, the author of many ideas and resolutions. It was his doing to implement the principle of dynastic seniority and seniority for pretenders, on the basis of which the descendants of Bonaparte had to resign their claim to the throne and concede to the Bourbons. It was he who brought about the election of an executive committee, made up of the crown prince, Albert Hapsburg, Rupert Wittelsbach and Nicholas Nikolayevich. And wasn't he the author of a proclamation to the peoples of Europe, a call to arms, in which Hermes Trismegista, the Apocalypse, Professor Teufelsdreck and many other authorities were cited:

> Monarchy is the sole refuge of culture and progress, the sole rock of authority, morality, the scale of the classes.
>
> Monarchy alone corresponds to the spirit and intellect of man with his aspirations to unity and his instinct for decorativeness.

Monarchy is the symbol of the collectivity, the personification of the unification and power of the people, it is the root of mysticism, it is the spinal column of history. Monarchy is the sash of tradition, continuity, majesty, religion. Monarchy is the only basis for justice. Monarchy is the only just system of distribution of material goods.

Monarchy is the sole defender of the proletariat, a representation of the battle and harmony of the classes.

Monarchy is the reduction of complex problems to simplicity, the order of hierarchy.

Monarchy is the rebirth of prosperity.

Only monarchy is able to defend European culture from an onslaught of Bolshevik barbarianism, from soulless American mechanization, from the anger of awakening Asiatic nationalisms.

Monarchy is the only panacea for our economic, political, social, moral, and philosophical ills.

Only the kings of peoples are capable of liberating Europe from the destructive yoke of the American kingpins of production.

Europe can choose: annihilation or monarchy.

The congress of monarchs, anticipating the senseless resistance and blindness of the peoples, poisoned with the venom of republican anarchy, resolves, sacrificing its pride, to nevertheless repay evil with good. It resolves therefore to resurrect monarchy wherever it does not exist, despite the momentary opposition of its subjects, for it assumes that the continuity of the monarchic tradition cannot be subject to interruption. In the meantime, far from their homelands, in exile, the anointed of all the nations will continue to exercise their complete powers, just as they had received them from their fathers and God, in order that the peoples, when they realize what they have done, will have a ready and efficient apparatus of power and authority without which they would face certain death in the dregs of anarchy. The sole just republic, the republic of kings in exile, will be a convincing model of the beneficence of the monarchic order.

8

The first and most important goal of the Executive Committee was to organize and secure a place for the republic of kings. This was an inordinately difficult task. A separate proclamation was issued to the League of Nations, in which, among other things, the Committee demanded that one of the countries of Central Europe be turned over to the kings. Ramsay Mac-Donald,* who together with the car given to him by his friend the confectioner had just moved into Downing Street for the second time, chaired the meeting of the League. (For in England each election brought victory to the Labour and Conservative Party, in its turn. The wise, farsighted gentility of English politicians resulted in each government's continuing the undertakings of its predecessors. Thanks to this the conservative government was socialist in essence, and by the same token the socialist was conservative.) After the proclamation was read, MacDonald gave a beautiful speech. He spoke about King Arthur and about the Knights of the Round Table, about the spirit of early Christianity, socialism, humanity, the attachment of the English people to the Prince of Wales, the frock coat, the New Jerusalem, the dawn of freedom, the dawn of peace, the hill of wisdom, the beneficial effect of sport on cultivation of the intellect, Monsalvat, and he ended with an enthusiastic paean to international brotherhood. The enraptured Geneva audience, that Olympics of oratory showmanship, that international Academy of Eloquence, showered him with applause. Then the delegate from North Africa, John Smith, an ex-ship's boy, currently the owner of tens of thousands of acres of pasture and farm lands, a coarse man oblivious to subtle European diplomatic arcana, steered the discussion onto completely different tracks. Alas, to the dissatisfaction of the dignified gathering, he dragged the matter under discussion out

*James Ramsay MacDonald (1866-1937) formed the first Labour government in England's history.—TRANS.

into the open in all of its nakedness and proposed that Paris be ceded to the kings.

9

In those days Paris was the City of Delight for the Anglo-Saxon race. Journey by air from England to Paris took a couple of hours. After a day of work enormous fleets of planes plied La Manche. Especially on Saturday afternoons masses of mechanical birds swarmed over the Channel like fish at spawning time. Lean, toothy Englishwomen would point out the few native French (hiding in the narrow rotting rooms of their houses and darting surreptitiously across streets) and would then peer into their Baedekers: "Frenchman: usually dark-haired, short, dirty weakling, hermit, etc." The virtuous sons and daughters of Old England, self-made men, gentlemen and sportsmen, leaving their phlegm, Bible, and Ten Commandments at home, dragged out their hidden instincts, eviscerated the stale, swollen-with-desire dregs of their subconscious, made animals of themselves and wallowed in open-air orgies in the Bois de Boulogne, in the musty caves of debauchery. Big-bellied native Americans fondled frail, Tanagra-shaped girls. Sadistic American women tormented Russians, those professional masochists. The French were cooped up between brothels under cover of ancient cathedrals and churches. In the summer, at dawn, pious processions—looked at with amazement by libertines returning from a long night out—emerged from over a hundred chapels and churches and quickly crossed the streets proclaiming their tender adoration of the Divine Mother in rapt canticles.

10

John Smith's proposal was laughed down. Instead, Councilor Seipel offered Vienna as the seat of the kings. But his proposal met with lively protest from the Little Entente and the perfidious Italians. The newspapers reported that Chicherin proposed the forming of a soviet of kings in the Crimea for the sum of two hundred million pounds.

11

At about the same time the papers reported the appearance of a new island in the Indian Ocean. Located east of Madagascar (between longitude 82-83° and latitude 12-15°) far from sea routes, it measured about 3,000 square kilometers. Surrounded by coral reefs, it constituted an almost inaccessible volcanic plateau, twelve hundred meters above sea level. Lying in the path of trade winds, the island possessed a wonderful, healthy climate and luxurious flora, and lent itself well to colonization. On the south side it was jagged, on the remaining three sides straight, so that it resembled a crown. The head of the scientific expedition that first landed on the island, a confirmed German monarchist, called it the Isle of the Kings.

Thomas Clark, who usually drew his inspiration and ideas from chance analogies, saw the finger of destiny in the name.

12

The exodus of the dethroned monarchs to the Isle of the Kings began in July of the following year. Multidecked steamers furrowed the Indian Ocean and delivered gold, old furniture, mistresses, architects, portraits of ancestors, music hall troupes, faithful butlers, counselors of state, officers, genealogical charts, tourists, film directors, aristocrats from all over the world, tailors, racehorses, engineers, exquisite chefs, automobiles, and land surveyors. The first thing the monarchs did was to divide the island into individual kingdoms in proportion to their prewar possessions. Thus Bourbon France gave up Alsace-Lorraine to Hohenzollern Germany. Borders were delineated; border checkpoints were set up and manned with gendarmes and banners.

A standing army of young blue bloods and imported globetrotters was created. The monarchs also built palaces—miniature imitations of capitals and courts, Parises, Berlins, Viennas, Versailles, Schönbrunns—with great creative enthusiasm and lightning speed. Military decorations and prewar constitutions were restored and parliaments and senates were called into session. And thus began a feast of life that had long been missing from human history: tottering, overflowing with delight, pleasure, and an excess of all things.

Impoverished Republican Europe looked with envy upon the cornucopia of the Isle of Kings.

13

In spite of the difficult access, contact with the island to the year 193- was unusually lively. From Europe came the marauders and argonauts of the aristocracy, dethroned kings, antique dealers, doctors who treated venereal disease, officers stripped of their rank, prostitutes, racers and cannons—everything that Europe had to dispose of. From America came morganatic wives of dethroned monarchs together with their dowries, canned goods, currency, wheat, meat, and surplus goods. In this way a few years passed imperceptibly—it was anticipated that exile would last but a few months. But the peoples of Europe did not see the error of their ways. On the contrary, the Isle of Kings welcomed more and more of the anointed: Italy's King Alphonse XIII; Yugoslavia's King Alexander; the Prince of Monaco; the Romanian King; the Sultans of Morocco; and Faisul, King of Iraq. Each additional invasion brought nothing but confusion and conflict to peaceful relations on the Island. The land had to be redivided, which caused border disputes and even armed skirmishes.

War—guardian angel of the thrones—accompanied a party of English emigrants on the steamship *Old England,* which brought the English court.

14

This was the last ruling dynasty on the continent and the last batch of emigrants. The gigantic steamship Old England delivered its passengers but never returned to its native harbors. It was smashed in a terrible cyclone that ravaged the Indian Ocean. It was also at this time that dangerous reefs and underwater cliffs surfaced around the Isle of the Kings, cutting it off from the world and eliminating all access to it for centuries. But this was not the only cause of the long isolation of the Island. The defeats and upheavals taking place all over the world were the focus of universal emotions and drew attention away from the remote island in the Indian Ocean. When, after ten years, calm was restored and someone recalled the lost exile of the kings, it was decided to forgo the search and let the whole matter be forgotten, so that new generations would remain ignorant of the concept and idea of monarchy.

It is only now that the real history of this out-of-the-way place, cut off from the world for centuries and harnassed irrevocably to the twilight of the history of monarchy, begins.

15

The history of the Isle of the Kings can barely be recreated in its most rudimentary outlines from the few surviving documents. As we have mentioned, the arrival of the English court dealt a profound blow to international relations on the island. The German Emperor Wilhelm II, fearing his role as leader would be undermined, concluded an anti-English alliance with the Hapsburgs. Wilhelm II acknowledged England's right only to land equaling the European territory of Great Britain, without taking into consideration its colonial possessions. He based his position on the fact that during the first division of the island the colonies of Germany, France, and Italy were not considered. The war which erupted as a result of the conflict between England, France and Russia, and Germany and Austria was almost a continuation of the Great War of 1914-18. In spite of the fact that it was shorter, it brought about profound losses in human life and in material and cultural acquisitions.

Peace, owing to the skill of English diplomacy (and most of all to the indefatigable efforts of Lloyd George), brought partial appeasement of England's demands, and in international politics, victory for a system that balanced the great powers.

16

One of the consequences of the war was a transformation in the system of governing the states. Owing to their isolation, the monarchs were liberated from having to espouse democracy, from having to set an example, from all administration and institutions which had been created as showpieces for distrustful peoples. The first strike at the constitution and parliamentary system, dealt by Czar Aleksey on the day of his coronation, had a detrimental effect on the remainder of the rulers.

Constitutional monarchy was transformed into absolutist monarchy.

17

Years, decades, centuries passed. The Isle of the Kings, cut off from the world, was plummeting into poverty; its culture and civilization were gradually disappearing. Poverty, absolutism, and militarism increased wars, and wars increased poverty and decline. Forced to satisfy their needs, the people began to specialize and differentiate themselves more and more and so broke down into three strata: the working folk, the army, and the court. The cities fell into disrepair, the palaces crumbled. The last remnants of knowledge slowly disappeared while superstitions and a militantly religious government took their place.

And just as at the close of the Middle Ages the discovery of new markets, revival of international relations, birth of capital, growing power of the cities, renaissance of humanistic culture, and development of lay science had transformed a feudal monarchy into an absolutist one; so now, in reverse, the isolation of the lost Isle of the Kings, its being cut off from the world for so many centuries, and the accompanying decline in its cities, capital, and science and reduction to a natural economy transformed an absolutist government into a feudal one.

18

The histories of the individual monarchies are difficult to reconstruct because of the small number and poor scientific value of the surviving historical documents. An example of this might be the biography of the French King Ludwig XXV (dated the end of the twenty-first century) which was written by a court historian in a strange, mangled French.

From it we learn that Ludwig XXV was a patron of the fine arts. He built a stable, whose beauty the chronicler sings in a lengthy panegyric, praising it as the eighth wonder of the world, a most beautiful work of architecture. The years of this monarch's reign, in the words of this court sycophant, constituted the golden age of French history. By all accounts, this illustrious period boasted victorious wars, which—as a result of the malice of the king's enemies—ended in defeat; wise governance, just courts, religiosity and mercy, gay court pageants, and beautiful women. Much space is devoted to this obsequious historian's descriptions of the great hunts, in which Ludwig XXV was an ardent participant, as well as the amorous jousts and feasts, of which he was a discriminating gourmet.

19

Relatively few of these documents have survived. We would find out very little that was interesting from the monotonous histories of the lives of the various Ludwigs, Karols, Fredericks, Richards, Alphonses, Emanuels, Johns, Wilhelms, Nicholases; or the history of the various war expeditions, plunderings, fratricides, treasons, murders, plots, violence, pageants, celebrations, hunts, invasions, superstitions, jousts, deaths, or plagues.

We are familiar with these things; a precise description can be found in any handbook of medieval history, if we read it backward.

20

Of the later documents, let us mention, for the sake of curiosity, a map which will give a concrete image of the disappearance of culture and tradition on the Isle of the Kings. It depicts the world as a circle of water with the Isle of the Kings, the only land, in the very center.

21

In the year 2431, Anarchasis Hualalai, a professor of history at the University of Hilo (Hawaii), ferreted out a reference to a vanished island that had appeared in the Indian Ocean in the twentieth century and was subsequently occupied by kings. According to the entry, the island had vanished in waves of oblivion in the aftermath of various oceanic and social cataclysms. That is why it was noted on only a few maps published at the time of its discovery and unknown until rediscovered this year by a professor digging around in old archives.

Professor Anarchasis organized a scientific expedition, made up chiefly of learned representatives of the black race (the professor was distinguished by an especially lustrous blackness and deep in his heart was extremely proud of it).

22

They set out in an enormous airship. After searching for a long time with no success, they suddenly came upon the island they were seeking. And when the black participants of the expedition trained their binoculars on the land stretched before them, they saw something quite out of the ordinary. Here on the naked plain stood several hundred whites gathered in a circle, clothed in animal skins and armed with long spears and shields. In the center a contest was underway between two hairy giants distinguished by an abundance and wealth of ornament and steel crowns on splendid red manes of hair. The shield of one of the wrestlers bore an insignia in which one could discern the crude outline of a lily, while the other shield bore the picture of a black eagle. In their hands the opponents held enormous javelins, which they manipulated and dodged with amazing agility.

Professor Anarchasis Hualalai watched them closely and then said to his black colleagues with characteristic solemnity:

"This is a typical scene in the life of barbarians: the outcome of the struggle between the chiefs resolves the dispute between the two tribes. From the emblems on the shields I would conclude that the King of the Franks is doing battle with the King of the Germans. Incidentally, now, as I watch them, I do not know how the whites could ever have prided themselves on the universality of their civilization, in contrast to us, blacks. If we were to rummage through every last corner of the earth, would we find even one black who was not basking in all the blessings of technology and culture? Never! Alas, these are observations out of their time. *We* know that not the color of one's skin, but the color of one's heart makes the man and that differences of race have long been obliterated. Now, gentlemen, the wearisome task of civilizing our civilizers awaits us."

————

THE HISTORY OF THE LAST REVOLUTION IN ENGLAND

Barely had the nervous, screaming Parisian stock market sputtered "Pound: 300" when a revolution broke out in England. Upon riding into what was usually a fairly empty street in the City, a clerk returning late from his relatives' cottage near London skidded and fell, smearing himself with something sticky and foul-smelling: blood. If he had not been late, if he had driven in twenty minutes earlier, he would most likely not be alive today: a fierce battle had raged in the streets of London. These were not crowds clashing with police, this was not a strike or even a general strike—it was a revolution! The first social revolution in England: armies of workers and the unemployed had poured in from the factory districts, from the industrial regions, from the provinces, a civil war, the red flag, blood. The heroically alert red eye of Moscow (red from sleeplessness as well) flickered with joy and hope: an international revolution! In Germany fear was stifled by the sweet hope of revenge. The franc—the powerless and defeated Carpentier got to his feet—would get stronger and return with a little extra punch. The mines of Upper Silesia and Dąbrowa thundered with a quickened pulse. Calm, phlegmatic Englishmen took to the streets in a stupor to examine the barricades, trenches, projectiles, and they understood nothing. And understanding nothing, they would die: in the rattle of machine-gun fire, in the onslaught of the front lines, in the strategy of street battles when the hissing projectiles—blasting holes, breaking windows, uprooting trees, lopping off treetops, toppling weak buildings, overturning buses, filling the air with gurgling, clatter, moans, commands, the internationale, and thunderclaps—sent the parchmentlike Anglo-Saxon souls of Englishmen who believed in the Bible, the King, and the Magna Carta into the afterworld.

On the morning of the third day the battle was concentrated on a narrow and insignificant street leading to the Parliament buildings. The success or failure of the revolution would be determined by the battle for this street. And a furious battle raged for two days. A mere few yards divided the enemies. The proles were attacking like lions. Police and army divisions defended themselves courageously. The vicissitudes of this battle will find historians who will not neglect to illuminate them exhaustively and universally, from all sides and positions. Even being aware of the involuntary distortions of the chroniclers in everything that concerns generalities, the amazingly absurd twisting of perspectives and false organization of facts into causes and effects, we feel obliged to objectively illuminate the mysterious finale of the last revolution in England (regardless of whether or not it will correspond to any ideology)—if not *ex visu et auditu* (as Swedenborg boasted in the subtitles of his works), then at least in the way we heard it from lips absolutely deserving of belief.

It happened thus. A freckled, lively Daniel Smith, while loading an ammunition belt into his outdated Maxim, suddenly saw a ball falling toward him from above—a bomb? shrapnel thrown from an airplane or from a window by some fanatic enemy of the proletariat? This master of the forward line on the workers' team in Lexington, a man who worshipped three things—social revolution in England, soccer, and large, healthy blondes—did not need long to think. He deflected the ball with an excellent maneuver in the direction of his opponents, in accordance with all the requirements of a good soccer game, of course. Must we go into detail except to say a certain Robin Smith, Police Officer No. 157 (who wore on his splendid torso, in between medals for courage, several medals for victory on the playing fields), claimed that he saw the bold and precise move of Daniel Smith? It is obvious that the cannonball, bomb, or shrapnel flew, dashed, and sailed from one army to the other, forgetting apparently where it was supposed to explode. It did not explode at all—it was not a cannonball or a bomb or shrapnel, but a normal soccer ball, which had wandered in no one knows how or where, sent by providence, as some claim; to illustrate the nonsense of historical chance, as others maintain; or simply thrown by some little tyke or crazy dreamer, who did not comprehend the enormous, almost cosmic weight of the contest for Great Britain, for the future of the world, for parliament, for MacDonald, for humanity, or for the king—as others would like.

The yelling of the furious trade unionists and the overwhelming lion's roar of British might continued. Missiles, bullets, projectiles fell, fighters fell, the cannonade boomed, salvos thundered, but a ball, an ordinary soccer ball, like so many others in sports shops, unremarkable in every way, a safe soccer ball threatening no one with anything sailed over the combatants, over the convolutions of battle, between the bloodied barricades, drawing more attention to itself, more passion and more heroic courage than deadly, dangerous bullets. Does it always have to be true in human history that the simple, safe, small, insignificant, worthless things excite more passion, kindle more courage, animosity, and heroism; arouse more interest and encourage greater effort than the dangerous, harmful, great, dignified, deadly things? So be it—we will say with great solemnity. If that is how things really are, we should be happy; for there are so many harmful and explosive and annihilating things that one should wish that humanity devote as little attention to them as possible.

Leaving these superfluous digressions to sworn historians, then, let us return to our barricades, where death, reaped with carbines and cannons, is not neglecting the rational sports culture of its lower extremities, either.

First Fred Cook got off the barricade. The blood of a born soccer player took over in him as soon as he saw the shot the police officers had missed. Paying no heed to the bullets which, whistling like innocent flies, stung harder than the tsetse and paying no heed to death, which in this instant knocked comrade

Tom, Police Officer No. 530, naval officer Milton Black, a student from Oxford, and volunteer Bob Clay from the scaffolding, the combatants, the people, and finally the soccer players began to climb down from the barricade smeared with red paste one by one and, as much as the narrowness of the street allowed, began to organize themselves into regular soccer teams. Harry Ball, a formidable speaker, the secretary of the union of leatherstitchers, the father of seven children, fell, without having had time to touch the ball with his raised leg. The ball was immediately picked up by a greater lover of whiskey than soccer, Ball's compatriot, Samuels. Barely had Captain George Lloyd bounced the ball off his head than it (the head not the ball) was pierced by the bullet of a Russian communist, delegate Trofim Aibeshetz. It was he, Trofim Abramowicz Aibeshetz, the lumen of the Comintern, it was he alone who with madness, with despair in his bulging, nearsighted eyes looked at the emotional *danse macabre* of death with the ball. In vain did he call to his comrades to come to their senses, to take advantage of the moment for a conclusive attack. Possessed by fury, he aimed at the accursed ball (and kept missing because of his extreme nearsightedness), until finally the mighty proletarian fist of comrade Daniel Smith brought him low and, in this way, with a truly English deed, documented the difference between a national and a nationalistic communism.

The shots were beginning to die down, the bullets were ceasing to cut the smoke-filled air, as if even they were becoming interested in the flight of the ordinary soccer ball. Hour after hour passed—the game continued with unflagging verve. The revolutionaries as well as the government side showed first-rate agility and skill, even more than earlier during the murdering. The advantage shifted from one side to the other, unable to make a decisive choice, due, perhaps, to the poor condition of the turf.

This lasted quite a while, until a certain (alas, nameless) player from the camp of the revolutionaries shot the ball so badly that it fell in the middle of the road and got stuck among the fallen. What should they do? The first man to move out for the ball, the theoretician of small medieval revolutionary movements, Max Weller (with a true-believer, Marxist beard), a peer-less dialectician and passionate hockey fan, fell right in front of the tangled ball after being shot by a corporal of the colonial armies who broke the ceasefire (and whose name, unfortunately, we are also unable to pass on to posterity). The next one who tried to get at the ball, a police officer, was felled by a proletarian bullet. Nine or ten boldhearted chaps lost their lives, their bodies lining both sides of the barricades right up to the ball. Once more, a penetrating historian might see some kind of symbol in this—but never mind what kind. It is enough that once again the cannons sounded, machine guns rattled and the life and death struggle, the harsh battle for prosperity, tradition, ideas, and revolution began anew.

In the meantime dusk had fallen; it was the evening of the second day. Throughout the entire night the thudding sounds continued, growing louder, then softer. The splendid courage of those fighting, itself worthy of a separate monograph, did not advance anyone's cause even an inch. The decisive moment of the fight was again put off to the next day and looked forward to impatiently by the tired, sleepless, famished combatants.

As soon as dawn broke and they saw—among the lifeless logs of corpses and the twisted bodies of the wounded, among hands stretched and frozen in movement—the ordinary, living rubber ball, whole and untouched, perfect in its round gray-ness—then, involuntarily, a joyous shout, a shout expressing an aroused instinct of self-preservation, the joy of life, a shout, which once must have greeted the sun after an eclipse, escaped from the breast of people weary with murdering, brutalized into a stubborn anger, hatred, deadly rancor, prejudice and the desire for blood—escaped from the breast of the police officers and communists alike. Joyous white flags appeared over both sides of the barricades, almost simultaneously.

An hour later two divisions, formed from the best soccer players, were marching toward the nearest playing field. They had decided to settle the battle for the street with a proper match. The losing side was to surrender unconditionally. Only a guard remained on the barricades to maintain order.

We could not find out, in spite of scrupulously conducted research, what the course of the match was or how many goals were kicked on each side. After an undoubtedly fierce and heated game—for the stakes were the fate of the entire world—the government forces won a smashing victory. This does not mean that the proletarian team had worse players—this must be stated and underscored. As luck would have it, the players on the police team simply played better as a team, and why not—how was Red Bob from Loughborough supposed to get together with towheaded Harold from Blackwall, or with bearded Black Tom from the Liverpool docks? Luck, chance, or historical necessity? Seek your answer to this question from philosophers of history. I simply wanted to tell you how the first, and, God willing, last revolution in England came to an end.

———

Has Anyone Seen Pigeon Street?

Something stranger than all the odd things at the Grand Guignol happened to Raphael. A street simply disappeared. The street where he had lived and where this morning he had left his wife and child. Pigeon Street. On the sixteenth of September, Raphael left the house at ten A.M. When he returned at three, he did not find the street in its place. It was gone. It had disappeared. Vanished.

Pigeon Street had the shape of the letter "T" (gallows and the first cross—as Raphael observed). The arms were dead ends, and the trunk was planted on Silver Street. At the foot of the cross of Pigeon Street rose buildings 18 and 20 Silver Street. The corners of the buildings, showing red brick gums through the gray gaping plaster, were the axles around which Raphael turned in leaving his house and returning there; they were the lips he walked into and out of. Now the lips had grown together, the apartments were grafted in an inseparable embrace.

Nothing else had changed. The passersby continued to pass, droshkies clattered and autos whizzed by. The sky was as gray as before and the horror of the everyday gave way to the horror of the inexplicable. He circled, stopped, looked for the missing street with anxious eyes, touched the unyielding hardness of the walls with his fingers, sometimes asking the passersby with a voice gone hoarse:

"Has anyone seen Pigeon Street?"

No. No one had seen it. No one had seen Pigeon Street.

How much time could have passed in this terrifying confusion? He did not know how he found himself at the police station.

Despair was consuming his heart. In vain did he want to rivet his stray pupils to the dusty molding of the window frame, to the dancing look of the chief, to the slanting ray of sunlight—his pupils and the molding, the chief's glance, and the slanting ray spun and spiraled uphill and vanished into bottomless abysses.

Where had Pigeon Street gone? To what mystical strata? Where were his wife and son, abducted by that chariot-street? In the overcrowded, shouting, and gesticulating world, what sort of awful and growing vacancy was this? In the tumult, in the hellish roar, what was this awful silence? The minutes bored into the pockmarked stone of his heart. Words slunk out of the corners of his mouth like snakes. They escaped from under the heavy stone of his heart. The shells of his ears became overgrown. The patter from the spiral stairwell echoed with the pounding of wild herds. Centuries long gone reverberated with a copper echo. Two men entered like destiny. Silence. A night of weariness will rock to sleep the despair, the shock, the longing, the whining fear curled up in the corner of his soul. The night of weariness—the starless black veil of Veronica.

He was led through the women's ward, because the entrance to the men's ward was being remodelled. A spacious, skimpily wooded garden. Fall. Curled leaves—gold, scattered horns of plenty. The sun was pricked with long golden needles. The melancholy of four in the afternoon. In the great room along walls dark with dampness, in the tumult and din listening to the voice of silence, old women with ashen faces sat on benches, with eyes concentrated on a vision in space. Immobile as the wooden frames of harmony, they enclosed from both sides the leaping, whirling, turning, jumping, clattering, snorting, jabbering, and crying of poor spasmodic bodies. Here and there, extended like axles, girls stretched themselves in immobility.

Raphael absorbed the misery of his surroundings, which shortly became a mystic consolation. He melted the misery into the pure gold of compassion. It spilled like blood, it became the rhythm of each atom of life and returned to Raphael vibrating like a bee, loaded with the honey of sadness, pulsating painfully.

Raphael's senses were open to every manifestation of life, wherever it came from, and they responded with the balsam of compassion. Compassion created its own, all-encompassing sense. It was the protective substance that the wounded organism of his soul secreted. The very existence of anything at all demanded redemption in Raphael's compassion. The compassion drew to itself, melted into unity, burned through the very principle of pain and existence—*principium individuationis*. Raphael's own sufferings became unreal as dried leaves in books; they were not the object of compassion—they were a gland that secreted compassion. Compassion was a cosmic feeling, it pulsated with the harmony of the spheres, it pulsated to the rhythm of the old man's running—this man, with whom Raphael lived, trotted from corner to corner, without respite, day and night; it transformed into angelic chords the ravings of the seventeen-year-old epileptic—his companion during walks in the garden; compassion devours the gloomy visions of that house of people—the comet of people knocked out of orbit—and smelted them into melodies. The most moving music, perhaps the only music, the harmony of the spheres—the melody of compassion took the stooping man, endlessly rocking and emitting sharp, birdlike sounds at regular intervals; the young man, searching on his bare knee for an infinite number of fictional parasites; the old woman with the inexpressibly sweet little face, petting the great gray cat, chattering endless tales to the two morose sons who came to visit her; the witch, with long gray curls, decked in motley-colored papers and rags, executing a witch's dance, shouting rhythmically wild, meaningless syllables; the horrifying, never-silenced cries of someone locked in isolation, the long passionate discussions conducted with himself.

When, after two weeks, he was set free, the disappearance of Pigeon Street, the disappearance of his wife and son, the terrible and real secret of the disappearance of Pigeon Street had moved into the realm of imagination. It was difficult for him to leave the hospital: here—rest, the simplified chaos of individuals, the monotonous tumult; there—anarchy at all levels, the crouching chaos of ill-boding surprises. The madness of souls was an island of peace and silence compared to the awful world of tangled secrets, compared to a world where suddenly streets disappear, where the madness of facts prevails.

And again the wanderings in search of the vanished street began. In the evenings, Raphael sat in a café by the window, where he could see the dividing line between buildings 18 and 20 Silver Street. At night on the floor of the café lay dirty, poor people, side by side, awaiting the beginning of work in nearby markets. Others threw dice, played cards, dominoes, under the sooty walls, under the dusty lithographs of the blind Samson or Hamlet. Reality gained contours, emphasized itself, grew to the tormenting clarity of a vision. Samson, smashing the pillars, the greasy king of spades with an ink stain on his crown, the faded, fly-dotted landscape took on the clarity of a vision, the epidermis of a realistic vision.

For Raphael's longing found distant dream landscapes under this outer skin. Raphael became a hunter, chasing the past, chasing the minutest details of the past on the sharp pavement of an empty Pigeon Street; rubbing up against the cracked facades of its old moldering buildings, wandering the courtyards dried up with dust, the smell of flies, junk, plaster, the wild faces and swollen dreams of childhood. He hunted remembrances, his son's blue smock with red polka dots, stained with fruit juice, the house in which he lived, covered with a roof of red slate—the notched beard of an Assyrian god. He tracked the details of his apartment along the walls of the café, where the electric light ducked under even lighter shadows. The birds on the wallpaper in the bedroom shrieked like birds in the forests of Ecuador, the headless Saint George from over the stove jabbed the vanquished dragon furiously with his spear, the dark flushing dampness spread like wild ferns. Each minute detail, each piece of furniture magnified its features and that which was his daily custom. The faces of things revealed the next planes of their visibility, each wrinkle, each wart, each color—only the faces of people, the face of his wife and son were veiled with the thick mourning of dusk.

There was no opportunity for understanding. Raphael's thoughts meandered in all the nooks of the natural and supernatural order of things. It was as if Pigeon Street had never been. But Pigeon Street—was everything, everything that was dearest, it was five years of life, of a most intensive life of love.

One evening in the café on Silver Street, out of an avalanche of dear, tender memories came strange words:

"Streets *must* disappear."—What sort of words were these? Whose? The fearsome words of Jehovah, cast from Mount Sinai? —No, only the words of a conversation, overheard in the Café on the Hill, the words of one of its frequenters, known to others as the "professor."

He remembered the rest of what was said: "Streets are prisons we are sentenced to live in together with hateful people; streets are straitjackets we put on every day and in which we wander aimlessly, seeking an exit in vain; Beata Beatrix is not awaiting us at every corner, blessing us with the palm leaves of her hands, nor is Rosa Mystica to lead us out of the chaos of coarse omnibuses and trams to the cities of angels; you sigh toward heaven in vain: heaven is the torn sash of a banner, draped over your grave of streets."

Raphael ran to the Café on the Hill. It rose on the hillside, with a view of the southern district of the city. A bower and a whitewashed house with a terrace were concealed in dense shrubbery. The owner of the café, which was considered a nest of anarchists and all types of dangerous demons, was an Armenian with crooked, bowed legs, reminiscent of the figures from Goya's cycle "Los Desastros."

Only one road led from the city: a very steep and narrow street, surrounded on both sides with high buildings. It ended on the hill in clumps of wild blackberries.

The professor and his friends were already sitting under a low chestnut tree. Raphael sat at a neighboring table. The professor was a tall, heavyset fifty-year-old guy with a beard pushing a belly before him like the wheelbarrow of life; he had a swollen face, blurred features, and tiny eyes that darted glances over his pince-nez. His voice had a metallic ring and his speech was like a crystal ball rolling downhill.

He was considered a dangerous anarchist in the district. People said that no one had ever been in his room, where he sat up nights preparing explosives capable of blowing up entire streets, bah, the entire city and who knows if not even the entire globe. The old crones complained about the laziness and apathy of the police, who reminded them too much, in this provincial town, of wooden police toys.

The professor tried to sit lightly in the frail, wicker chair. Among his friends was a certain poet, who twenty years ago had published a twenty- or thirty-page volume of poetry and who found answers to all the problems of the world in this or that verse on this or that page of his forgotten book. There was also the hemorrhoidal, yellowish friend of a certain critic, the apostle of a religio-anarchist society, a society of free and independent religious villages, a mystical Catholicism of free parishes, isolated from the Roman hierarchy; a former revolutionary, who lived on the memories of his youth and returned to them with tenderness, praising the past with all of its contents, including the czarist regime; an art dealer, pornographer, newly arrived from Paris and living at the rectory of his acquaintance, a parish priest, in a home opening onto a garden, fragrant with dried apple skins and the heat of decaying earth; a painter, who always lamented not having become a social activist in his youth; a judge, who meted out severe sentences while pondering the Absolute.

Raphael listened to their conversation:

"The café is a monastery à *rebours*. A monastery in which man seeks intimacy with man and in which he finds loneliness a hundred times more lonely than an Egyptian desert. Never and nowhere else have I felt the degree of absolute isolation of human existence that I did one night on the fourteenth of July in a fashionable café on Montparnasse, full of dandies, adventure- and money-seekers, coquettes, artists, savage foreigners, panting, yes, panting with an unconcealable restlessness of loneliness that was growing more naked, accursed, frightening and mad with each concealment, each amusement, each escapade and licentious act. You might also find an occasional hermit there, delecting in isolation among the shining crush of faces, like a miser, tasting the delight of poverty among the flashing gold of coins."

This tirade was delivered by the former poet, the author of a completely undistinguished volume of poems.

"The café," the painter who regretted not becoming a social activist said after a short pause, "is an institution that is better than a prison, in guaranteeing peace among governments. The café is a mill that grinds to husks of words the flaming heads of heresiarchs, revolutionaries, and dangerous types that break out of the confinement of social norms. Here people with destructive and creative instincts and anarchic temperaments drown the unconquered armadas of revolt in cups of black coffee and in the narcotics of an artificial paradise, change the bullets of words capable of igniting a revolution, into the clinking copper of intoxicating conversations with friends. Close the cafés, scatter these people; and the world . . ."

Raphael could not hear the last whispered words.

"The café," said the art dealer/pornographer, who saw sex in everything, "is the only and noisiest transformer of the revolutionary libido, one of the concentrated ties, in which the changing, I would say, moulting sexual instinct currently crystallizes its centers of gravity. In smashing monistic social forms, monism, monogamy, monotheism, and monarchy, in dissolving family chains, in overturning in a frenzy of dancing the seemingly untouched norms of social morality, in dragging out all of man's monstrous complexity, in mixing together races, sexes, concepts, religions, civilizations, drinks, in unleashing a jazz band of customs and infusing poetry with homosexuality and neo-Catholicism, by unveiling itself in an exhibitionist outburst in all of its omnipresent, all-encompassing nakedness, and by washing over the modern day with perversity and psychosis— the rebelling libido seeks a new balance, a pluralistic, relativistic balance. Brothels are no longer just the isolated gutters of forces deviating from utilitarian social norms—today they are creative arteries, fortifying all the lymph nodes of life. The café, I claim, is one of the halls of the universal bordello of the world, it is one of the stages of removing the bed from the crannies of the marital boudoir to a public forum. (Apropos, I am reminded of the stone bed on the square in Leiden on which Jan from Leiden copulated with his twelve female apostles—and we, too, are the heretics of a religion as yet unknown.) The café is a function of the brothel, just as the drawing room was a function of the family. I realized the role of the café many years ago when in an obscure small teahouse on Rymarska Street, I was served a pastry in the shape of a phallus."

The sun's purple condensed in the west. The pornographer stopped talking, because he noticed that the professor was drumming his fingers impatiently on the tabletop. This was a sign that the professor wished to speak.

"As for me," the professor said and the crystal ball of his voice rolled down the hill of his stomach, "I think that the café is the promise of unemployment, a new actionless society, the ultima Thule of laziness. The blessed tent of inaction, the blessed lamb among the wild beasts of the city, cars, skyscrapers, needlessly whirling haste, and superfluous work. The café is a respite from a productive worldview and a productive world, it is the blossoming senselessness of existence, it is a temple of the intellect in a world of mechanical thinking. The living source of miracles, legends, and modern apocrypha. A paradise of misanthropy. Here in the café man grows distant from man with a speed faster than the speed of light. Here space disappears; here there is no continuity. And here we learn to hate man. I would like," he added after a moment of silence and looking toward the west, where the sun had gotten tangled in the bushes like the hair of Absalom, "I would like the earth, this planet, this footstool under us, to disappear without a trace, to blow away into nothing, so that only our Hillside of Wisdom survived, and we upon it, talking about the things of the annihilated earth against the backdrop of a red curtain, hiding other worlds, which, unfortunately, it is impossible to annihilate!"

Silence. The evening star was pinned to the sky like a poster. Insects chirped in the grass, timidly, invitingly. Raphael brushed away the moths of memories, the bats of memories, tangled in his hair, the evenings of childhood, thick in the gray shadow, still, overhanging with dread and sweet melancholy. Night fell, the greasy gloom of night. Raphael's suspicions, timid as the chirping of the insects, robed themselves in certainty. If there was someone responsible for the disappearance of Pigeon Street, then it could only be God or the professor. His words, his tirades full of hatred toward the streets, toward the world, full of misanthropy, were the first distinct clues to the missing street. The magic of its disappearance confirmed Raphael's thought that there is no thing so fantastic or so impossible that it cannot come true. Who was the professor really? Wasn't it possible that under the guise of a buffoon, a talkative vagrant, lurked a mighty and malicious demon, a wizard of modernity, a brilliant inventor? Technology! This word took the place of magic, miracle, a miracle not noticed because it was common. This splendid unleashing of miracles and surprises! While the world spins along its cruelly regular circle, while the earth turns on its axis, while day follows night and night day, while people outline an ordinary chart of their lives, interrupted by the small perturbations of dramas and deaths, who knows if in some small town, in a small room some strange buffoon was not devising an invention that would stop the rotations of the earth, that would blow the earth into a myriad of small planetoids, that would magically erase the spaces, that would tear a shoulder of this or that street from the living organism of a city without even leaving a scar? The professor, generally considered to be a dangerous man, could have been the inventor of some brilliant way of magically annihilating space! This was surely he! Raphael felt an irrepressible longing for his wife and child, cast by the professor's magic into what abysses of being or unbeing?

He decided to track down the professor, to tear his secret from him and to find the antidote which would resurrect his street, his building, and his loved ones. This was all that he could do, perhaps the thread was false, but it was the only one he had.

Raphael had often read about suicide squads, excellently organized, having at their disposal the enormous wealth of some maharaja or other, the pens of wonderful writers, and a far-reaching, effective propaganda. He had read about secret societies bent on destroying European civilization, about mass arson in Berlin, the epidemic of cannibalism and sectarianism, about the violent decrease in births, about the thousands of manifestations of destructive acts, suicidal instincts, or perhaps the activity of some powerful secret organization for the annihilation of the world. Perhaps here in this small town, peripheral to Europe, beat the heart of a criminal plot. In that case, his quiet, secret fight with the professor was the battle of Ahura Mazda with Ahriman, God's fight with Lucifer. The stake—the existence of the world. The field of battle: the cross of Pigeon Street! The symbols and metaphors donned living flesh.

A few days passed. Raphael left the professor only at night at the entrance to his apartment building. He followed him all over the city, accompanied him to the taverns and cafés, watched him carefully and discreetly. Moments of complete doubt alternated with moments of absolute certainty. He wavered in contradictory feelings between the despair of resignation and the anger of zealous battle.

One afternoon—in the cool fall air the scorching sun followed him like a companion—he saw the hard contours of objects under the bulky cape of the professor. Raphael assumed they were some sort of destructive apparatus. Indifferent to his own safety, he decided to find out. He ran ahead of the professor a few steps, turned quickly and ran into him so hard that the mysterious things fell out from under his coat. Unfortunately? happily? these turned out to be nothing more than books. Both the pursued and the pursuer bent over to pick up the scattered volumes. The instant the professor saw Raphael close up, he realized that Raphael was following him.

The professor's joy was short-lived, the joy of flattered ambition was crushed by the tank of fear. The professor was terrified, convinced that Raphael was a secret agent. He decided to run away, but he couldn't gather his skittering thoughts. Losing presence of mind, he circled the city, mingled with dense crowds, sneaked along back alleys, hid in entryways and finally was able to lose his pursuer. Then he ran to the house of a friend, a former revolutionary. However, this former expert on escapes and battles with the police was so aghast when he found out about the professor's bad luck that he gave the professor some advice that even the professor thought was incredible and then pushed him out the door, arranging to meet him at the usual hour at the Café on the Hill.

The professor decided to flee to America. He went home, packed up the essentials, underwear, clothes, an old portrait of a woman, a white silk scarf, a few papers and books (among others, the Bible disguised as the pornographic *Le jardin parfum*), colorful, old-fashioned ties; he sneaked out timidly, got in a droshky, and was driven to the Café on the Hill. But none of the professor's friends were in the café—this was the first time he had been here at this hour in many years. The professor waited a few minutes and then in another attack of panic decided to leave the city at once.

At exactly the instant that the professor stood at the top of the narrow, steep little street, Raphael was walking up the hill with eyes cast down to the pavement. The stones were sharp, polished by rain and shoes—exactly like those on his unfortunate Pigeon Street. Raphael looked up just for a second but that was enough to make him stop dead in his tracks. A vision or reality? The professor was coming downhill, obese, enormous, wide, and behind him—emptiness, nothingness, nothingness, radiant with the glow of the sunset. Surely it must have been an optical illusion, excited by the narrowness of the steep street, but Raphael didn't know that.

He knew just one thing: that the demon of death who annihilates everything behind him was coming toward him! He was coming closer, in a moment he would pass Raphael, and then Raphael would stop existing, just as Pigeon Street had stopped existing. His feet froze into stone, he closed his eyes and waited for the end.

In the meantime, the professor came running downhill, seeing nothing before him. His excitement, his feeling of haste, magnified his usual nearsightedness. He recognized Raphael only at the instant of collision.

The strong blow tore Raphael out of his lifeless expectation. The blow of ultimate annihilation! He opened his eyes automatically. And, seeing before him the wide, indistinct face of the perpetrator of his misfortunes, Raphael suddenly boiled over with hatred, sorrow, anger. He grabbed the professor by the shoulder, shook him and said desperately:

"Street, wife!"

"Pardon me," mumbled the professor, flushed, "but what do you mean?"

Raphael did not find Pigeon Street, because it never existed in that town (nor will you ever find the town on any map. Nevertheless, does that make the disappearance of Pigeon Street less of a mysterious riddle?). He did not find his wife or child because they, too, never existed. Raphael was a known bluffer and spinner of tall tales. Now, for example, it is Sunday evening. Raphael is sitting on the veranda of the Rotunda. Through the clouds of smoke rising from his cigarette he imagines dramatized heretical landscapes.

Aᴘʀɪʟ ꜰᴏᴏʟ

Peter Moreau spent the after-dinner hours in an armchair, pondering the superiority of order and system over anarchy, humor, and all spirits of revolt.

These were not empty sophistries, bereft of essential contents—no! All of Peter's long life was the best confirmation of these thoughts, an unceasing demonstration, a splendid apotheosis!

The long life of Peter Moreau, all his days, exactly alike and systematic, made him blissfully aware of order, an awareness of a precisely executed plan, compared to which the misfortunes of old age, weariness, and all the powerlessness of a worn-out body are nothing!

All of his days!—only . . . one single, different, incomprehensible day eluded the rigorous column, filling Peter with a strange sense of excitement and anxiety. It was becoming focused in his memory now as in a film, growing, growing beyond measure, threatening to eclipse, threatening to destroy the fine order of his long life.

On 31 March 1921 (decades had passed, but Peter remembered this day precisely), librarian Peter Moreau was returning from work at the usual hour. Contrary to his daily habit, he stopped along the way home and sat on a bench in a square. This first deviation from the Regular Plan of the day was undoubtedly the beginning of the derailment, of the unusual and strange catastrophe that was to follow.

It is most likely that Peter had acquiesced to this deviation under the subconscious influence of the first day of spring. It rushed into Paris, tearing away the skinny bone-cold winter and the postwar insufficiencies. The city, remembering well the days when it had been the terrible shrapnel of destruction, bursting with the fragments of human millions onto the fronts, now transformed itself into a grazing, whistling shrapnel of joy. It seemed that any minute it would explode the gay adventurous company of things animate and inanimate, that it would tear them into joyous pieces and send them to embrace the sky, that motley, stupidly gaping sky, looking like a young Junker.

But twilight was approaching and the sky was growing bluer and bluer, gleaming with steel flashes, which pierced the gentleness, the solemn sweetness of the weather with a strange magic. The street melted into dusk, similar to the loveliest aquafortis saturated with quivering light and shadow. Airplanes fluttered overhead like angels, rising in the sky in the shape of a cross. Over them—the pink lilies of clouds and the full red heart of the sky, a heart moving into the shadows, a heart weary with love. Beneath them—the drowsy swishing of trams and the colored processions of cars and vehicles. But above all it was the scent, the scent of Primavera which moved one to the quick, and the twittering sparrow orchestra, which hung like papilla from the stately old age of the tree—still black with winter.

And in this sleepy langorous movement of sky, vehicles, and lights, in these immobile, massive canyons of stone, sky, asphalt, the colored, thousand-headed, thousand-armed, thousand-legged mass fell, rose, swelled, pushed, rubbed, divided, spilled, exploded joyously, shouting and laughing.

In the meantime Peter stopped existing as the Peter Moreau he had been, the learned librarian. Torn from him was the shell of dull mechanical gravity, torn away were the transmissions of habit, which herded him without respite into the machine of the Daily Plan; regularity, order, accuracy, system, responsibility, and the precision of the marvelously functioning watch disappeared and blew away. What remained was: the unformed living heart of emotions, perceptions, and impressions, a blossoming avalanche, the living principle of blossoming itself, of smell, shape, color, play of light and shadow, movement, and the joy of the street.

It made no difference which of the many comical episodes, served up to us so abundantly by the filmstrip of the street, of a particularly Parisian spring, became the pattern of his nascent consciousness and gave shape to a fluid and already coagulating sensitivity; which of these silly accidents, phenomena, amusing situations, these involuntary Chaplinades with which the sophisticated and trained eye is capable of amusing itself endlessly, fell into his consciousness so forcefully that it become exclusively the consciousness of comicality.

It is enough that up to now Peter was completely deprived of a sense of humor. Peter, who had probably never laughed, now in a sudden change saw the world surrounding him as a mushrooming, whirling organism of comedy.

He was given to fits of laughter, a geyser of laughter, he became covered with its mobile, undulating musculature. He did not particularly need comic situations; each situation, each detail, each visible fragment was already a source of humor: stone objects, people, in the tangle of their movement and stillness. The almighty law of humor now ruled everything.

"Comicality is the incursion of the imaginings of superior life forms into the lower, just as tragedy is the reverse phenomenon. It is the guiding spirit of the human race, a principle of culture, a sprouting upward, a racing toward more and more perfect forms. In this understanding, for example, the superficially contradictory tendencies of contemporary literature become comprehensible: humor and the striving toward religion. What, after all, is contemporary religion, if not a justification of the rushing toward higher forms, a justification which nothing else can provide? From this perspective, humor becomes a method; contents, religiosity, and mystification become a revelation! Seen this way, mountains of old misunderstandings explode! The misunderstandings of chaplains, who did not know that the soul of religion is not a mystified revelation, but a revealed mystification; the misunderstanding of philosophers who, in unmasking revelation as a mystification, did not notice that mystification *is* revelation."

This is what Peter Moreau would think if he could and wanted to think at this moment. But he was so occupied with experiencing the world anew, in the element of laughter, that he had completely forgotten about himself, he had forgotten about the sacred long-lived tradition of the ritual of his life.

It was after midnight when car lights and a garish poster enticed him to attend the evening theater. *Landru, Murderer of Women* was playing. This was a skillfully recreated abridgment of the famous Landru affair, which for several months nourished Paris and the entire world with a shiver of sensation and enriched the gallery of today's types with an interesting type of modern Bluebeard.

Landru was accused of murdering and robbing seven women. Adopting various ploys—buying furniture, proposing marriage—he would establish intimate relationships. The only real evidence of his crime was the disappearance of these women and a few charred bones, found in the small kitchen of his villa.

The play was enormously popular. Peter, who had an orchestra seat right next to the stage, found much joy in the two-way mystification of actors and audience that is the basis of theater. Here the mystery plays of mystification took place; here one learned to know its charm.

An execution was supposed to take place in the epilogue. The guillotine was already positioned on stage. The public followed the action of the play. Suddenly, when the attention of the viewers reached its apex, someone from the orchestra seats jumped the divider separating the audience from the stage and stood by the guillotine: "Landru is innocent. I am the murderer!" he said in a deep and moving voice. It was Peter Moreau.

Soon Peter's authoritative and suggestive voice overcame the uproar and thundered over the absolute silence.

One must realize that what Peter said next found listeners even too grateful and receptive. For many reasons. The naïveté of the theater audience resulted in its not noticing that Peter was acting and moving as if he were an actor in the play. With its characteristic awareness and sense of wholeness, the crowd passed from the imaginative world of the theater into the world of concrete reality, not seeing the untraveled and unplumbed chasm that divided them.

Next—the whole issue was confusing: perhaps because the theater cult for deviant heroes is contradictory in its essence, as people honor them for their deviations yet desire their rehabilitation; or because the faith in theater as the voice of the conscience (Hamlet) elicits a response in the most hardened criminal, for who would be capable of bearing the terrible sight of his crime twice as heinous because it was paid for with the blood of someone wrongly sentenced? Or perhaps because of the profound, albeit warped, faith in immortality, a faith which cannot reconcile itself to death as the final, all-resolving judge; as well as the subconscious hatred in each of us for the court and the joy of confirming court errors—this and many other factors prepared an arena that was very comfortable for Peter, who in these circumstances effected a splendid apotheosis of mystification.

His mimicry was convincing through its violent pain, expressed by his transformation of internal laughter into external tragedy. He spoke in the silence with a completely passionate voice, sometimes raised and whistling, sometimes muffled, as if it were emanating from the profoundest depths of his soul, where remorse lives and man coexists with God.

"What made me a prisoner of this man, whose moral inferiority always filled me with disgust? I don't know how to answer. Some harsh and vicious law told me to strive for my own defeat, it told me, just as it does a swallow caught in a cobra's gaze, to throw myself blindly into the gaping jaws of destruction. Landru ruled me with a cobra's gaze, with the stare of a magnetist . . .

"What would a man be without deception? Deception is the only morality acceptable to man, the beast in which all the holiness of heaven and all the villainy of hell are bound inextricably. But even in a world where the principle of all choice, the substratum, the indispensable condition of morality is hypocrisy, even in this world, how repulsively, how perversely, how deceptively, how terribly hypocritical is your lofty, your holiest, most ideal word, the word friendship! The word you use to mask in a cowardly way the brutal cannibalism of your souls, your civilized cannibalism, that essence of your vital forces, raised to the ideal of parasitism. Why, I was Landru's friend!

"He singled me out very early, he sought me out with his rapacious instinct and marked me to be a victim. The unbalanced passions, which tore at me and threw me onto the hostile and alien waves of life, made me fine and easy plunder. Landru put my alertness to sleep, he flattered me, won me over with his obsequiousness and friendship. And when he finally drew in the net—I was defenseless. Then he became my tyrant, the master of my every deed, my soul and body. Then came the hell of a terrible agony, disgraceful dependence, revulsion toward myself, revolt and the hatred of a prisoner, which does not dare reveal itself.

"Landru had the character of a vulgar bully, the beguiling charm of a salesman, and a sophisticated, albeit barren, intelligence. Perhaps he even loved me in the way one loves a victim. He needed me; I was a condition of his existence. From me he drew energy, inspiration, strength, even life. Left to himself he was nothing, he would not exist at all; grafted onto someone else's will, he developed and blossomed luxuriantly. He was a virtuoso of deceit. In me he raised for himself the executor of his criminal plans. I committed all kinds of villainy—cheating, extortion, spying—without even realizing it. I, who had always prided myself on an overly sensitive conscience, lost all sense of transgression, since it was inspired by him. I plunged lower and lower. As years passed resignation set in. To the world, to strangers, I was a miserable creature tolerated thanks only to the generosity of the noble Landru. In the eyes of strangers, my virtues were transferred to him in some peculiar way, while I was weighed down with his vices, his vulgarity, his animal egotism, his unusual greed. His presence was enough for me to lose the last shreds of good will that were left to me. I was the object of general and, above all, my own scorn and revulsion. Having exhausted me completely, he broke off all my ties with the world.

He took away my close, well-wishing friends. And soon he alone was my sole link to the outside world.

"But Anna was my inner life.

"It began with her. I hid her from him for a long time, and I dreaded the moment when he would discover her. I knew that he would do everything to take her away from me. In the duel for the woman, the victory was predictable. How I trembled at the very thought that he would see her, that he would recognize her. I hid her carefully. I hid her for a long time. Long enough for my love, the love of an isolated and debased man, to burst into flame, to burn me to ashes; long enough it seemed to me, naive as I was, to be certain of her love. What naïveté to be certain of a woman's love. I dreamed that here, in this great passion, I would be reborn, that here I would revive and free myself from the torment of disgraceful imprisonment. What foolishness! I was building my rebirth on the faithfulness of a woman! Finally he found us out. Everything went much more quickly than I could have expected. He invited us for a Sunday walk on the outskirts of town. I did not want to go, I had forebodings about what would follow, I was nevertheless weak enough and indecisive enough to give in to her pleas. Disgraceful weakness.

"Everything happened quickly after that. I have to admit, he knew how to be charming, witty, subtle. In a café on the outskirts of town where he took us, I noticed in their eyes those involuntary flashes, that almost magic tide of mutual attraction, that mystical flame so divine for lovers and so terrifying when it burns in the eyes of one's beloved for someone else.

"They were awful, cruel moments—centuries. I didn't know how to cope with it. Paralyzed, deafened, I knew only one thing—that he was taking her away. I was powerless, defenseless, immobile from inner tumult. Everything was falling down on my head, melting, getting bogged down in a swamp of agony. I couldn't bear it any longer. I had to hasten the catastrophe. I don't know what I did, I don't remember. I don't know. I remember only that they left together, spattering me with their contempt.

"From that moment I never left them. I was the shadow of their love, I watched the sated contentment of their happiness. I was always by their side, I devoured the sight of their caresses. And they did not avoid me—it seemed that revealing their most secret caresses of love in front of me supplied them with the most refined pleasure.

"Until one night—numb with pain, I slipped into their bedroom with a kitchen knife in my hand . . .

"We said not a word to each other. Landru shook in feverish terror. I should tell you that this bully was an extraordinary coward. He fainted at the sight of blood.

"In complete silence, we occupied ourselves with cleaning up all clues to the crime. A crime until now that you did not know about . . .

"It is stuffy in here!"

In a thoughtful silence the audience carried Peter out into the street.

Nothing broke the almost devout silence except a late droshky clattering along somewhere; the milky blue lamps and the light of the stars illuminated Peter and his voice thundered, growing and diminishing with strange emotional modulations.

"Now everything was changed, was reversed entirely.

"It was I who was the ruthless, brutal tyrant—and he was afraid of me, he trembled before me like a slave before a cruel god. Murder immediately gave me an advantage, a clear-cut, absolute advantage. With laughter, with an awful convulsive laughter, I sometimes caught his gaze; formerly, ah! it was so terribly contemptuous, now it was following me surreptitiously, in worry, in frozen adoration.

"He did not turn me in—I knew too much about him. I tormented him, I reduced him to tears, to attacks of hysteria. His fear grew with each day. He wanted to escape. In vain. Luck had turned its back on him. He began to fail. He dreamed of escaping to America. He became an obedient tool in my hands. He began vulgar blackmail, he bilked lonely women out of money, women to whom he had promised marriage, the purchase of furniture and property. I waited until he formed close relationships—then I appeared, I the tormentor. I was jealous of those old, ugly, and ridiculous women! I persecuted them, I treated them brutally. In vain did they seek protection in his then perhaps honest goodness, gentleness. He was powerless.

"There were always three of us in the spacious villa where we experienced the most awful moments of our life. Revenge, I was burning with revenge, heavens of revenge and triumph, for all the years of oppression, feverishly mad heavens of rapture opened up for me. How I tormented that poor pair, with what delight I savored each terrified beat of their hearts! What a terrifying night! Exactly what happened to Anna repeated itself . . . Landru screamed, it seemed to me that he had gone crazy. We kept busy with the stove . . . We carefully removed all traces . . . After this crime came others. Other crimes followed with terrifying regularity. Landru no longer attempted to escape. Perhaps the narcotic of crime had drawn him in just as it had me. There was no force to oppose it . . .

"His death was the last bit of blackmail. He did not turn me in. He alone wanted to remain—the exclusive, secret hero of the great crimes. After all, how could it have helped him to implicate me: his conscience was heavy enough. The desire for popularity and theatrical immortality is stronger in these people than the torments of real death! . . ."

The crowd was in an unusually excitable mood. At Peter's request, they carried him in their arms to the prefecture. Here he identified himself. When he stood on the steps once again, the crowd shuddered with curiosity. "I am not a murderer of women. I am the prophet of a New Jerusalem." They listened to him dumbfounded. Peter would not come to his senses. He shouted, struck his breast, cried. He called on them to do penance. The Last Judgment is near! The cup is overflowing with sin! Only harsh penance and prayer can save the world from annihilation. O depths of human depravity! He had to tell them that fairy tale about Landru, because otherwise they would not have listened to him. (Worthy of amazement is the consistency with which the spirit of deception that overcame Peter, struck at the pillars of society: at justice and religion, those rigid pillars, which the human spirit had burdened and undermined with the unnecessary ornaments of doubts and dialectics.)

He despaired, shouted, implored. The crowd was infected with the religious mood. A sensational prophet can always sway the populace, and in these postwar times the mob was religious. The street awaited its Vernard de Clairvaux. Skeptics stepped aside, afraid of the dangerous and enthusiastic exaltation. Women responded with cries, spasms, and moans. Corporations of Catholic youth appeared, illuminating the street with torches and filling it with pious song. Dawn spread a fan of grim colors that cooled the fanatical faces. In religious admiration, as if on a miraculous pilgrimage, they poured through the streets, carrying Peter on their shoulders.

They sang. Sins were publicly confessed. People mortified themselves. Converted Magdalenes confessed their perversions. He led them to his house, where, as he told them, he had gathered the symbols and instruments of mortal sins. Like Savonarola, he desired to surrender them to the mercy of flames.

Day was breaking as they approached their destination. Peter disappeared into his apartment. A moment later, he shouted from the balcony, "Brothers, sisters, I've been robbed."

The crowd was breaking up grimly and apathetically. Dawn crawled off the roofs and higher stories and angrily cast lifeless, cold colors onto the huddled human shapes. The student fraternities left in fours, singing songs. The sky was already touched with a colorful, gentle warmth. The birds twittered.

Newspaper vendors were filling the street with shouts: "Landru is innocent! Apprehension of the real Bluebeard!"

At that very moment Peter Moreau was looking at the wrinkled face of his old housekeeper, which was twisted into a question mark.

Then involuntarily his eye passed to the calendar: "April Fool," he said in a monotone. And then, looking at the old wall clock, whose dial with Roman numerals leaned out derisively from the gaping mouth of a satyr, he added:

"Why, it's past time for my morning tea."

Hermaphrodite

O strange irony of existence,
In which faith is faith
In illusion.
O strange power of faith, which
Is the mother of existence.

Conversations of Jan Olbork
With His Soul

1

Perverse irony or chance had formed Peter's exterior in the most complete contradiction to his true nature. A vigorous bearing, features that were one hundred percent masculine, and the face of the ideal male were prodigal gifts for this *pur sang*, if I may say so, corporeal and spiritual hermaphrodite. What a source of constant, absurd mistakes! Oh, the feminine wooing and fervent emotion, comic in their futility, that Peter, the involuntary Don Juan, brought forth from the hardest rock of virtue!

An example? Mrs. Cleopatra Van Hymenseel fainted when she saw Peter for the first time at a small neighborhood restaurant, The Quiet Father's. She saw in him the image of the cruel deity to whom her life was an unending sacrifice. But let us leave her be until she crosses our path again as the unfortunate heroine of this very strange story.

Peter was a hermaphrodite not merely in the flesh. I will not describe what sort of "castration" or "Oedipal" complex constituted his absolute psychological sexlessness in childhood. If I pandered to theories of pansexuality fashionable today, I would deny Peter that which we label, correctly or incorrectly, as the soul. No, I will not be cruel toward my hero: I will not deny him a sensitive and even Romantic soul, a subtle intelligence capable of emotional rapture.

The riches accumulated by the ancestors of his race allowed him to lead a life of leisure, and to spend it in endless travel to faraway places. A contemplative mind and a temperament deprived of sensuality justify the label of vagrant philosopher, a label which I would most gladly apply to his social role. A category of people, thank goodness, dying out today. Peter's thoughts about the world were, rather, fragments of unobligatory thoughts about a world from which the sexual element had been extracted and in which the reflexes acted in place of energy. The laziness of daydreams, walks, books, sleep, hunting, trips and adventures—the present moment of a sexless sybarite washed gently without obstruction into the past, into the smoke of childhood memories, into the foggy landscape of his youth, redolent with cruelly blossoming apple trees, the sweet looks of his mother, a heavy and damp sky, a compressed space, from which one would like to sail away on the bloody ships of dawn under smoky, fluttering masts of clouds, into the copper of the falling night, into the gloomy lyceum, whitewashed hallways, hospital smell, the feisty old-fashioned shadows of teachers with strange boatlike coiffures; into the fragrant thickets of gardens, into purple rains, stuffy violet grottoes, where on all fours he gave rides to his little pal and taskmaster, a heavyset Frenchman from Cairo, a wild little bull with red cabbage roses for cheeks, to whom Peter yielded one cruel stormy night—all of this was lapping against the shores of his consciousness with the calm rising and falling of waves of passionless enjoyment.

Today we meet him in that city, which during the day is a city of pursuit of money, the gambling roulette of work, while at night it is the city of Venus. Peter lived in an out-of-the-way hotel called the Inn of the Wild Voyages on a remote street. A small building in the shape of a pigeon's roost, plastered with wild grapevines and innumerable bird nests. From the windows of the room, covered with a red checkered curtain, Peter saw before him a dark green, rain-soaked Gothic palace covered with the patina of old age. Old age leveled all allegories; the sooty virtues, some with twisted heads, did not differ in the least from the twisted grimaces of mortal sins. A tram at the bottom made its way through a narrow street like a red windup toy and stopped right in front of the store At Padishah's. Whenever Peter looked out on the street and into the enormous window of the store he saw the double-chinned proprietress, immobile as a barbarian idol, smiling at him coquettishly with one bright eye. Whenever he went out for a walk he was followed by the stares of women (their eyes brimming with desire) who tried in vain to muddle the passive joy of his life.

> Fatum est in partibus illis,
> quas sinus abscondit: nam si tibi
> sidera cessent nil faciet longi
> mensura incognita nervi.*
>
> Juvenal, *Saturnalia;* cited from Montaigne:
> *Essais,* Book 3, ch. V.

The only man with whom Peter was friends in this city was his neighbor from the hotel, Hamilkar Pater. Their travels gave them grist for their long conversations and joined them in a bond of disinterested friendship. How peculiar! Hamilkar was the exact opposite of Peter. Sensual to the marrow, masculine, he had something in himself, in his look and behavior, something indefinable, which repelled women and resulted in not one (as he claimed) wanting to succumb to him, even for money.

Hamilkar told Peter his gloomy and extremely peculiar amorous adventures.

---

*"There is a destiny that rules the parts our clothes conceal; for if the stars abhor you, unheard-of length of member will do nothing for you."

Hamilkar's First Tale

This is one of Hamilkar's tales.

As far as my memory reaches, I find in myself an unsatisfied desire for both love and holiness, joined together, like the steeds in Plato's metaphor, one of which pulls you toward the heavens while the other drags you to the ground. In the fourth year of life I put my hungry lips to a puddle left behind by a nasty companion of my games. At six, sleeping with my sisters, I feverishly waited for them to fall asleep so that I could surrender myself to timid attempts at ecstasy. At thirteen, I almost went out of my mind with desire. At eighteen, in a metaphysical desire for purity, I mortified my flesh, surrendered to ascetic practices, wore a hair shirt, and struggled with an enemy of the law of the species which considered itself my more real "self." Lying on the couch for hours I dreamed about the bellies of women, about the damp vegetation of Venus's mound, about breasts swollen with heat; I wallowed in the imaginary debauchery of bodies. Feminine shapes became the archetypes of all shapes. The red of genitals contemplated in paraoptic vision became primal red, the Platonic idea of colors. The body of a woman realized in desire was the abc of all impressions, observations, and their transcendental a priori form—like space and time.

I subjected myself to voluntary fasting. In the summer, tormented by heat, hunger, desire, burning with lust, I wandered for hours all over the city—a modern Dante in an inferno of desires. I was tempted by the rustling satins of prostitutes, the pitiable indigence, the sweet fetidness of their swaying on the corners, it teased me with its sticky heat, in which loomed the dampness of sweaty female breasts; I was tormented by the animal, perspiring summer evenings, with lips, the meat of women in carriages, the swaying buttocks of women walking, the extreme smiles of legs, the blossoming, sweet fragrance of virginity. The open doors of restaurants attracted my hunger, their dense, meaty odors, cold nightmares of lights, heatwaves of sumptuous undressings, the devilishly sexual melancholy of their music. For hours I stood before the public toilets out of which women came and went, I stood in front of urinals, sweeter than the sweetest virginal boudoirs. I—the ravenous, augmenting temptation by jingling coins in my pockets—I was drawn by stands with soda water and fruit, waited on by fat, healthy girls in whose blushes I recognized an excess of blood, faint menstrual secretions, the healthy release of debauchery.

One summer evening I was sitting on a rock overlooking the great river winding around my hometown. This was the third evening of my voluntary fast. I was thoroughly exhausted with hunger, the heat of the sun, and my unrelenting desire. A happy coincidence brought a woman to the rock where I was sitting. What did she look like? She was a woman. A wide, flat and small forty-year-old cow. A hard, dense piece of fat, bluntly shaped. Greedy, lustful and mean glances dribbled from the slits of her eyes on her fat greasy face, colored with beet juice. The small upturned snout of a nose was an unexpected addition to the puffy cheeks. A wide bust stiffened beneath the crepe blouse painted with flowers; her breasts were the two broad handles of the swollen pitcher of her belly. It was from this pitcher that I wanted my first strong draft of sex; it was from this pitcher that I wanted to intoxicate myself with that fiery drink of sensuality that I had craved for so long. From this pitcher decked out by what fetishist in a little cap with an enormous butterfly of ribbons and brown lampshade of a skirt? From this pitcher which irritated me with its revolting smell—the mildewy cleanliness of frequent washings, dress shields, cheap-smelling soaps and, most of all, the unbearable smell of the sacristy, the smell of piety—which to this day fills me with an aggressive nauseousness.

We understood one another almost without words. After barely a minute, we were walking arm in arm to a certain isolated spot she knew under the viaduct. Dusk was upon us. She pinched me as we walked and from time to time she mumbled: "You're a skinny one, angel." I was indeed very skinny at the time. A thin, sad angel, starving for his downfall in the arms of a sow. I whispered something with lips dry with hunger and emotion; I was trembling all over. It was completely dark when we reached the desired place. Then she submitted me to one last search through my clothing. The result was discouraging. She hesitated. "It's not worth doing with such a skinny guy"— she finally said. She left. Left, leaving me in inhuman agony.

That was my first romance. Woman revealed herself to me then in all of her monstrous nakedness: she was a she-spider, feeling her male before devouring him.

Hamilkar's Second Tale

The café where I spent my evenings had a doorman who was a skinny, frail fellow, a hairless nincompoop in his thirties with a thin, broken soprano voice. It is difficult to describe the daily agony of this man, who, being a passionate smoker and cigarette vendor, could not smoke because of the mindless prohibition of the café owner, a woman (fat as a Buddha) eternally sitting not far from the entrance behind the counter of the cash register. It was on these stuffy summer evenings, when there was no one in the café except for me and a few more diehard lonelies and when the obese owner dozed, that this modern Tantalus could stand outside the glass doors and smoke on the sly, holding a cigarette in his fist like a soldier on watch; he smoked passionately and deeply and quickly burned up a dozen cigarettes. On these occasions, outside the doors there stood a ragged, fifteen-year-old girl who hung around fashionable places; she was dirty, bespittled, a revolting cretin, a beggar, kissing the hands of all passersby and casually selling matches, newspapers, and her miserable degenerate body to cabdrivers impatient with the long wait or to elegant, refined gourmets of the repulsive. Pressing her face to the glass, she stared at the doorman with wonder, with humble admiration in her murky fish eyes. Who can describe the delights experienced by these two: the man surrounded by the light smoke of satisfied desire and the woman, adoring him as if he were God, gazing at him ecstatically, frozen in blissful fulfillment, in Nirvana, *nunc stans.* In what ecstasies they both wallowed, ecstasies known perhaps only to a select few in the Middle Ages and worthy of the envy of the most tender lovers. This went on for two months, each evening until eleven o'clock, when the café began to fill up with people. Unfortunately, everything must end and all love must pass. It ended one summer when the owner of the café died and the doorman received permission to smoke.

All of Hamilkar's tales were similar to these, odd and unnatural.

Peter's room was next to a room rented by the hour. Through a hole drilled in the door by some lascivious predecessor, Peter watched the frenzy of bodies coupling in the most various combinations, monsters in the image of Hindu gods, made up of many appendages. They remained puzzles whose true meaning was completely inaccessible to him.

"For me, this riddle," said Hamilkar, "is all too intelligible. For me this riddle is the basis of all understanding. The whole world seems to be this puzzle to me and life a fiery sex act. When, lying on the bed, I look at the belltower, I see: a stiff phallus, tearing apart the softness of clouds.

"Actually, I see it everywhere, that hard victorious fetish, before whom I weep, small and tired."

2

Phoenix ex cinere reviviscam*

In walks along the lanes of a beautiful cemetery, cities of stone, where sorrowing trees advertised the silence of rock with their rustle, in walks along alleys, along countless streets Peter had been meeting, for some time now, a woman in whom he recognized the heroine of the fainting incident at The Quiet Father's.

*Phoenix, I will rise from the ashes.

Sometimes, when leaving the hotel, he saw her waiting on the other side of the street; she would mask the embarrassment and uneasiness of her wait with the poorly imitated ease of a woman who is waiting for a tram and looking in a store window.

Finally one evening she approached Peter. The tiny murmur of rain or kisses of timid words. Then the ascending, concentrated crystal voice of passion.

The history of her life was sadder than words could tell. Her youth had passed in one of those stone crates of the business districts of the city, where people differ from boxes of merchandise only in manifesting greater motion. She was hated by her father, an evil, paralyzed old man who did not believe he was her father, and who, powerless and neglected, did not leave his bed and swore furiously in the pauses between his moaning. He was neglected by her mother who rarely peeked in and so, alone, afraid, abandoned, eternally hungry, she wandered aimlessly along the empty rooms wrapped in cobwebs, hiding her fear in the dust on the windows or in the corner of her room. Sometimes her mother brought home jangling and noisy firemen from across the street. In her parents' bedroom at night the sleepless Cleopatra heard the inhuman groans of her father, rising on a wave of helpless, boundless fury; the curses and abuse of the firemen; and the licentious whinnying of her mother.

When she was fifteen, a private tutor acquainted her with love games without depriving her of her virginity. After the death of her mother, she married the first man to come along and propose: her much older cousin. He was incapable of making a woman of her. Nor did he lament this; he was content with his feeble efforts. He got married because he was incapable of becoming attached to dogs, or in any particularly strong way to money. He did not think about her feelings, nor did he even think that she had any.

One morning Cleopatra, profoundly irritated, met an older neighbor woman, the widow of a fine writer, in the common bathroom. Cleopatra surrendered to her caresses, to the subtle practices of female caresses according to the ritual of Lesbos.

The relationship lasted a few months, that is, until Cleopatra saw Peter at The Quiet Father's.

What could possibly happen to a barrier of shyness and timidity, to a paper barrier when the burning ink of desire spills over it? What could possibly happen to a body, a woman's body, a man's body, a human body, the flask in which wine changes to vinegar; that bottle of impurity, from which demons and fretters drink passionately in what invisible inns of space? What could possibly happen to the human body when it is consumed by the fire of love? What could possibly happen to lips, the slot in the money-box of the heart, to the heart itself, that poisonous Pandora's box, nest of nightmares, drum, pillow of desires?

Cleopatra spent all her evenings with Peter. A lightness unknown to her until now, a joyous lightness overcame her and banished the dull burden of passions that had oppressed her throughout her life. It seemed that the enormity of the passion which directed her toward Peter, now, under the influence of his presence, changed into the tranquil joy of friendly relations. But shortly thereafter everything changed. Cleopatra entered an inferno of anguish, in contrast to which her earlier sufferings had been mere purgatory. Leaning against his shoulder, feeling his closeness, she fell a hundred times in the course of one moment, she plunged into the torpidity of martyrdom, from which return was a miracle. Forgetting about her pride, about her bashfulness, and paying no attention to Peter's passionless attitude towards her, she gave him a hundred proofs of her love. In vain. Each step was accompanied by the keen desire to have the earth vanish from beneath her feet and, at the same time, by the desire for an immediate escape—to flee from him, to surrender herself to the first man that came along! To flee from him, to surrender herself to the first man that came along? There were no men besides Peter, there was no escaping him. His indifference fixed her with a nail of despair, a nail that pierced right through her and that stifled even her cry, the cry of a dying woman.

Peter's attitude toward Cleopatra was passive. In spite of her many tokens of love, he was unaware of her passion for quite some time. He met with her because she desired it, because she appealed to him as a companion on his walks. If he noticed her pain, why, didn't even he know that pain is a natural state for millions of people? He simply tried not to see it, just as one does not look at the ugly view outside a train window. What can a speeding train do about the ugliness of the view? The only thing it can do is not stop its movement. Peter did not stop the movement of his life up to now at the sight of Cleopatra's sufferings.

In the malignity of the day, in dreams, in which his appearance deprived her of the consciousness of a dream, the thought of him, the taste of his presence was everything; it was an arc between dreaming and waking—the bitter continuation of her dream. If it was the thought about him, then it was the thought of every cell in her body, hungering for Peter as if he were air. Each moment of her almost vegetable life beyond Peter emanated from him like a negative, like a secondary imperfect reflection of him, like a minor existence drawn out of the enormity of his nebula.

Senseless and beaten, in bed or at the window, fixing her hair or browsing through a book—it was Peter who lifted his hand to her hair, he who filled the unintelligible paragraphs of the books she was reading with music. The long hours of the day were a prayer to hasten the evening, to hasten the moment when she would see him. Then, at their meeting, the fog surrounding him sunk into the hard outline of his figure, into the angles of his movements, into the chinks of his melodious voice. She felt this with exposed nerves, with her skin turned inside out. Each moment in which he did not love her was killing her, devastating her—an enormous, awful injustice, which would never be set right, the sin of lost time, which would never be recovered. And when her pain, her anger and her inner turbulence reached their highest pitch, then only the gentle touch of Peter's hand, only his look changed them into tearful, thunderous enthusiasm, into the warm rain of crying after a storm of emotions, into a humble, slavish idolatry.

The road, the streets by which he walked her home became an everyday Calvary. The unsatisfied desire, the sorrow at parting, the emptiness of the hours that awaited her alone in unconsoled inner weeping rose from the depths of her soul up to the nave of the heavens, fueling its black abyss with a dangerous whirlwind of defeat. The heavens grew deeper, the street more distant, the passersby smaller—before her stretched a lonely road, a Golgotha of monstrous agony. In order not to vanish in them altogether, she clutched at lifeless and indifferent things which, like stations of our Lord's suffering, became a source of joy, the light of unearthly consolation. A cigar hanging over a tobacco warehouse; a generator eternally pounding with the murmuring prayer of reassurances; the delicate fresh greenery, like soft streaming hair caressing the light of the gas lantern, spoke to her with a boundless mercy and induced tranquility with the caress of forgotten childhood lullabies.

Having spent her life in an intense atmosphere of sexual frustration, Cleopatra had nevertheless maintained her virginity, her cloister-like purity and virtue. But now—this was something else. This was a mission, a revelation, sent from the heavens, an angel with a phallic sword!

In her dreams she breathed him. Awake, in moments of falling asleep and waking, on her lips, in her eyes, over her entire body she felt him in excessive wonder, she felt him as the only reality of her soul, as the only contents of her consciousness. He was no longer contained in any one sense. He had melted them all into one mighty superhuman sense of love.

Even in hours of extreme exhaustion, in moments of complete weakness, the perspectives of new raptures tore through, just as the street along which they walked constantly revealed the new vantage points of its cross-streets.

Then again an orchis of desires, of instincts would reawaken, sorrows would flood and drown her expiring consciousness. Her restlessness rose on the rhythms of his words, on the rhythms of his male voice, like a frail boat on the thrashing waves of an ocean that will consume it.

Against Peter's will she moved into his room. She left her husband. She did not leave Peter's side; she watched him to make sure he did not run away. She tormented him with the tyranny of her love. Because he refused to sleep with her, because he intended to leave her, she would spend sleepless nights on the couch, half-undressed. She despised and idolized him by turns. She accused him of intentional cruelty and sadism, of planning to maltreat her and then, in turn, she would suffer pangs of conscience.

The madness of a woman's love tore out the rails from under the speeding train. Peter understood the nearness of the catastrophe. He neither could nor wanted to reveal to Cleopatra the secret of his indifference. He could not out of regard for her. For he knew that the loss of her faith might kill her, the loss of faith in a life that was so full of illusions, a loss of faith in his manliness, which was only an illusion.

Cleopatra now begged only for his pity. She could not understand his behavior. Finally, she gave in to her fate. What could she do? But what a painful sight, what terrible torment! Exhausted by the madness of the situation, Peter could barely restrain his tears when he looked at her at night, curled up, tossed by fever, waking in moans, similar to those which she had once heard from the lips of her father.

She agreed to her fate. And what is more, she understood it, she believed in its ruthless necessity, in its inexorable logic. In the painful vision of her tormented flesh, she understood that the cruel god who kindles insatiable desire in human bodies is himself ideally cold, ideally indifferent. The coolness, the indifference of Peter raised his manliness even higher, somewhere into divine strata, and made him a god, the pitiless god phallus.

Peter saw salvation only in escape. Could he leave her though? He pitied and wanted to help her.

He wrote a letter to Hamilkar begging him and coaxing him to return, to get him out of a snare from which he was incapable of extricating himself. But Hamilkar was gamboling in the pampas of Uruguay and adventure-seeking in the company of hardy, fearless trappers.

The days passed tediously. After the stormy ones came peaceful, exhausted, torpid ones. Fall worked in their favor, peeking into windows with a cold, gray sky. Even the heart of a hermaphrodite is a flower pot in which love may suddenly send out a few shoots. Peter barely understood the deep-seated changes which were occurring in him. His blood pulsated differently, the invisible cocoon in which he had been wrapped until now was dissolving. Love for Cleopatra tore through his feeling of pity. Sometimes in the evening, in the armchair, in which they both spent the long hours of the day lost in a drowsy delirium, his half-closed eyes studied her features, made to stand out in a luminous line against the window, he looked at her stiff and depressed form, he looked at her with a look in which she might have discerned the traces of desire from which she was dying. Peter's desire was emerging from him just as the first germ of love had issued from primal silt, just as the world had emerged from the astounded demiurge.

He could not recall how one evening he suddenly found himself at her side. The piercing cry of a woman was the last thing he remembered before his deep, unconscious fall somewhere into a bottomless abyss.

> Salomae interroganti: "quousque
> vigebit mors?" Dominus: "quoadusque"
> inquit "vos, mulieres paritis" hoc est
> quoamdiu operabuntur cupiditates.*
>
> Clemens Alex. Stromata, 9.

Peter did not notice that he had impregnated a dead woman. Her heart had burst.

The life and death of Cleopatra is reminiscent of the lives of many blessed and saintly women. She died like a saint, to whom God had revealed himself, God, in agony, summoned by superhuman degradation; God, created by her faith, zeal, was forced to reveal himself because of the strength of her faith. Her days and nights, practically translucent with ecstasies, how do they differ from the religious ecstasies of St. Teresa? While remembering Tertullian's words that the devil is God's ape, we are,

---

*To Salome, who asked: "How long will death last?," God replied, "As long as you women give birth," that is, as long as desire exists.

nevertheless, careful and this story, which we might be inclined to receive as a legend about one of the Lord's saints, we would rather consider to be a story of a saint of diabolical forces.

The life of Peter-the-man after Cleopatra's death is the subject for another story—a story about a Don Juan, which I will write some other time. Sometimes it seemed to Peter that what he had experienced possessed only the reality of a dream, that it was an illusory reality, like that possessed by sources shooting out of holy grottoes, where the Queen of the Heavens appears to poor shepherd children. This deceptive reality is the only one (it seems to us, the unbelievers) that faith is capable of creating.

At such moments, however, Peter's hand, like the hand of doubting Thomas, wandered over his body and testified to the ruthless reality of the incredible transformation.

LONG LIVE EUROPE!

(from the Memoirs of an Ex-European)

I loved her more than any woman. I repeated her name hundreds of times. I got choked up just thinking about her. All my passions and unfulfilled dreams of childhood and youth melted into one great overflowing love of: Europe.

And maybe that is why the only friends I ever had were Jusuf ben Mchim, a huge, dark Somalian, and a Chinese, Chang Wu Pei, a student of mathematics. I taught them love for a land where every inch was fertilized with genius, plowed with sweat and blood, magnified with heroism, spiritualized. I taught them to worship Europe, that great eternal Europe which, after centuries of toil, was climbing endless rungs of contradictions and antinomies, shooting toward the heavens with the religiosity of its virtue and vice, bursting with the momentum of progress, bonded by dynamism in every one of its atoms, its creative, productive tradition speeding in eternal restlessness from unity to complexity, from multiplicity to simplicity.

Often my friends and I would stand in front of the jewelry store on the corner of boulevard des Capucines and rue du 4-Septembre and I would take in the wondrous view of the European masses. Leaning against a wall, in wild inspiration, I showed them that masterpiece of historical selection—the European, whose heroism is no longer a deed but something as natural as breathing. I showed them a people in which highly favorable centuries concentrated all the culture, sealed all the greatness and downfalls of humanity in a synchronistic orchestration without peer. I showed them women with elongated spines, like the spine of Saint Peter Moissac, chattering midinettes and models, chargers of the Bastille from whose eyes, circled with a nimbus of dark pencil, beamed the passionate faith of Joan of Arc. I showed them the Odysseuses of finance, the English, in whom the current of revolutionary mysticism had stiffened into orthodoxy; Jews, the business agents of Europe, the schlemiels of Europe, who sold their shadows for thirty pieces of silver; the proletariat, whose steps thundered in indomitable will and power; the whole crowd, energetic, joyous, deeply creative. As in Hoffman's wonderful tale "Elixirs of the Devil," where every pattern of stones inevitably formed the shape of the cross, so this crowd, too, so varied, so incessantly active, incessantly developing, always formed just one shape: Europe.

The war broke out but didn't succeed in stifling my enthusiasm. My friend the Somalian enlisted in the French army out of love for Europe and fell in the first skirmish. Chang Wu Pei left Europe and I lost contact with him. I knew only that he had returned to his homeland. I remained alone, participated in long marches, rotted away in the filth and clay of the trenches, fought in five battles, was wounded three times, lost my right hand and finally, with joyous enthusiasm, greeted the convalescence of peace.

I know historical upheavals occur independently of individuals, but still I cannot rid myself of the thought that I was the one responsible for the terrible cataclysm that befell Europe, that I am the one responsible although my name is not nor ever will be found in a single history textbook. If not for me—I often say to myself—my friend Chang Wu Pei would have spent all his life in *analysis situs,* a geometry of position, and would have sat poring over books into old age at some university on the North American continent to which he had had the intention of emigrating. It was I, me, with my thoughtless apologias who inspired in him a strange and fanatical degree of adoration of Europe and Chinese patriotism. Could I have suspected that in the frail, shy, and neurasthenic son of a coolie from Liu-ting there slumbered a Napoleon of the Orient, a Peter the Great of China? It was my enthusiastic tirades that stirred him and returned him to his homeland, which, if it had not been for them, would still be in a state of lethargy, or at best would have awakened, but later, ten, twenty or a hundred years later, but not then, not at the very moment when Europe, torn, anarchic, overcome by a momentary, yes, a *momentary* suicidal rage, became easy plunder that seemed to beg for a conqueror.

Then came the year 193-, that unforgettable, terrifying year. We remember the lightning speed of the surprise Mongol attack. Immense Chinese armies, well-organized and equipped with modern weapons, marched, victorious, across Europe, meeting resistance nowhere except in Poland, which true to its knightly tradition lay down a bloody sacrifice in uneven battle. Almost simultaneously, the Chinese were seen in Warsaw, Vienna, Berlin, Paris, Rome, Madrid. Crazy with pain, I watched as white marauders plundered and burned the Louvre. An hour later, on the wide and empty rue La Fayette, I spotted the entering Chinese cavalry. Numb with despair I reached for my revolver with my left hand and, closing my eyes, fired several rounds. I remember nothing after that. I fainted.

I came to in a train car. We were deported, all of us, all the natives of Europe: we were scattered over the great expanses of Eurasia, in proportions carefully calculated, among the barbarian peoples. We were to have the same mission as the conquered Greeks had in Roman times: we were all supposed to become teachers.

I was taken to Jun-nan, a small village carved out of loess. I remember my first lecture. It was as if a fog veiled my eyes: all the faces of my Chinese pupils blended into one nightmarish face, a repulsive mask of Notre Dame gargoyles. A voice, hoarse with hatred and revulsion, shouted through my lips: LONG LIVE EUROPE!

Twenty years passed, enough time to get used to any situation. I fulfilled my obligations conscientiously and led the dull, listless life of a recluse. I watched the development and speedy civilizing of the little village I lived in with distrust. I noticed it but it never penetrated my consciousness. One morning, however, when an official brought me orders to return to Europe, to Paris—I was not happy about it in the least. On the contrary, I felt old wounds opening that had been healed by the balm of time. I did not want to see, I did not want to see her abused, ruined, overrun by barbarians.

I returned by dirigible. As soon as I got to my destination, I made my way quickly to the assigned apartment. I hurried through the streets with downcast eyes. I didn't want to look but I could not help seeing an exuberant urban civilization. All the worse, I thought: a top hat on the mangy head of a cannibal, the lifeless shell of a form, the Americanism of yellow savages. I would rather have seen ruins.

I didn't leave the house all that day, but on the next a policeman came for me and took me away under escort. A car was waiting. It took us to the corner of some street. The policeman told me to get out. I looked around—ah, it was the well-known corner of boulevard des Capucines! Memories assaulted me in a searing wave of blood that burst upon my brain. In the tangle, in the knot of memories and emotions, I suddenly felt an arm on my shoulder. I turned around: it was my old friend, the former student of mathematics, Chang Wu Pei, now the dictator of Eurasia, the great conqueror of Europe, the reformer of China. I recognized his muted voice which spoke to me now of greatness, of heroism and creative impetus, about the productive instinct, the centuries-old culture, about the rich orchestration of contradictions, about the selection of tradition, about the virtue and vice of Europe! Chang Wu Pei was showing me the passing crowd, alive and vibrant, breathing heroism and revolutionary momentum, bursting with creative dynamism, energetic, that wonderful masterpiece of historical selection—the European!

And indeed, here after forty years, on the same street corner, with the same friend, I had rediscovered the same Europe, blossoming endlessly in a thousand forms, complex and simple, holy and criminal, nihilistic and full of faith, revolutionary and orthodox and inspired: eternal, eternal, immortal Europe! It was as if scales which I had been wearing for twenty years suddenly dropped from my eyes! I looked more keenly, carefully at the crowd that was passing us: I saw the same figures, the same faces, the same reflection of inherited genius, the same flash of intelligence, the same uneasiness, the same, the same faces, only a little yellowed—with time? Like the aged and yellowed pages of a book?

Chang Wu Pei was no longer with me. I stood lost in contemplation, where all thought dies, where reason ends, where revelation appears, when I was torn out of it, torn out by a passerby—I recognized a former pupil of mine from Jun-nan—who had been staring at me a few seconds and who, smiling with his slanted eyes, cried out: LONG LIVE EUROPE!

TOM BILL: HEAVYWEIGHT CHAMPION

Then I spotted him, a tragically downcast athlete in those sad surroundings, whose gloom was varnished by the broiling heat— a heavy dense inkblot of a heatwave, spreading slowly as if out of the opening of an inkpot—from the sun of an August afternoon.

Sitting on a low, dark wall in a courtyard on rue Monjol, full of weeds, wildly growing grasses, rotting garbage and scraps, large fearless cats, the soot of a blackened trashheap, coal, children—whose purity and grave, quiet games created the impression of grime, manure, and a real and painful poverty—Tom Bill was warming the neglected, long-unshaven, haggard face of a man mortally exhausted. In the center of the courtyard on a tall heap of rubbish, crumbled plaster, old iron and excrement, Tom's dog—a mangy old brown hound with a leprosy of white spots on his back and a wounded, pockmarked snout—also warmed himself in the sun without moving.

Somewhat farther down the street, a two-story building, a slab of sick stone, sootcovered, blackened, eaten away by dampness, was caving in, crumbling, with windows and doors twisted into a slant. Holes riddled this stone the way they did a rotting tooth: the hole on the ground floor was the apartment of a prostitute who was sitting on the step; patched laundry—the rags of the risen Lazarus in old paintings—was hung out to dry on a line in the second hole; in the third, on the second floor, a smiling young girl was bent over a washtub; and the fourth hole was a gaping slit, cut in two by a narrow board.

In front of the building on the other side of the wall the earth dropped sharply for a few meters—at the bottom craters, hills of sand, potholes with puddles, the foundations of the newly rising (*comfort moderne*) tenements, machines, piles of wood, many-storied layers of girders (reminding one of the illustrations in geography textbooks representing the virgin forests of South America with cowboys looking out from between the trees); water dripping from the concrete foundation, workers, iron, the music of saws, the grating clatter of metal—the splendid rousing voices of work; farther down was the dense construction of high, convex Parisian roofs of gray rock mass, and farthest, at the very end—Montmartre hill, with its deliciously cold and pagan Sacre Coeur—its white triumphant rock.

Over it protruded an alien blue sky and a scorching heat beat down from the sun—the fever of excitement, from the opening through which that old dissolute voyeur of poverty—God—peeks down at us.

One reaches Monjol by way of steep steps from the rue Asseline. Here, having looked through the window into the black interior of the only inn, I saw a few persons, arranged around a table—a genre scene of conferring criminals, seen in dreams, in the daydreams of childhood, in old naive books. Here, having looked in through the open doors into the black interiors gaping with a squalor showing the wood rot of its interiors and barely covered with the rag of an old poster of Concert Mayol or Cadum soaps, I saw wide, made beds, vanities, framed photos, maybe even the photos of strange families, oil paintings of naked women, the timid pornography of kisses and poses—the frozen, pretentious decorations of impoverished prostitution. In front of these openings, in which hung torn curtains, holy faded rags taking the place of doors, sit women in bathrobes, on chairs, on stools, mainly old women, decaying, hunched, wrinkled, with a book or some handiwork, silent, calling to the rare passerby or chatting with one another. (At midnight on the unlit lanes of Monjol and Asseline naked old women emerge from the rubble like enormous, grayhaired cats, running across the street with the lit stubs of candles, shielded by the bright shell of a palm.) Rue Monjol is more crumbled and dilapidated, the women here are older and even more immobile, the landscape is more congealed and the idyllic prostitution of the old streets is more melancholy.

On that August afternoon the three of us sat sad and still on the low wall of rue Monjol, listening to the voices of work, listening to the grate and swish of saws, the ripple of water and the clanging of metal: I, Tom Bill, and his dog. From noon to the setting of the sun. Then just as heavily and as slowly as the sun, he got off the wall and, limping, dragged himself toward the entrance of the shabby building. I recognized in him the brutal athlete whom I had seen a few months earlier in a bar on rue Marcadet, and about whom a few months later a long-haired Russian anarchist told me stories in a dirty bistro on rue Bolivar.

Tom Bill was thirty-six when he took a serious account of his life. He assessed all positions severely and impartially and concluded: minus, loss, absolute bankruptcy, a complete vacuum. A reader, especially a reader accustomed to detailed psychological analyses, will probably want to know what inclined this thick-skinned wrestler, this zealous professional of the most brutal fights who barely knew his multiplication tables, to make such a complex and dangerous reckoning. This is an interesting question, it is true, but unfortunately the author is unable to give a satisfactory answer. First of all, he is no psychologist and, if he has written this story, it is only because the grim figure of its protagonist visited him incessantly, like Pirandello's characters, during sleepless Parisian nights of longing; secondly, the author is accustomed to an almost daily reckoning, like a careful book vendor, of the losses and gains of his conscience and really has no idea what compels one to take an account of things only once every thirty-six years. In order to make this assignment easier, let us say simply that the spring of the active life of the athlete Tom Bill was wound only to that fatal year thirty-six. Let us not deny, however, that the real reason could have been hidden in some accident, even in some accidental freak of a street chronicle, in the banal and tolerated tragedy of the everyday; or, lastly, in some insistent thought or psychological complex concealed until now. It is enough that here the life of the celebrated, victorious, universally merciless, lone, heavyweight champion Tom Bill who sowed fear in the hearts of even unknown passersby ends and a new life, difficult to describe, not lending itself to description, full of the biting rust of malignant reflections, lyrical returns to childhood, infections of undetermined longing, which are capable of eating through even the most steel-like girders of muscles, begins. Could it be that the layers of lyricism born of loneliness and a difficult childhood, in demanding an outlet, an outlet in a pure crystalline wellspring of inspirations or in the besmirched geyser of boiling passions, had drilled a path for themselves straight to his heart—that crater where atavisms wrestle with the weakness of an individual—washing over them with their waters, full of the silt of daydreams and the mussels of childhood? Tom Bill immediately discovered new maps of life. His memories began to glimmer through the real facts of the day, as if through transparent Japanese screens. He still fought in the arena, ate in restaurants, trained, had a woman and a Bock beer everyday in the bar on rue Marcadet, where I spotted him sitting on a tall stool one summer evening (and where a short, rotund, and gabby bartender with an unpleasantly naked face told me after Tom Bill left the myriad details of his cruelty; animal ferocity; grim, heavy, inhuman character; his maltreatment of his opponents; and his famous double Nelson, which meted almost instant death to the young, likable, and promising Ludwig Chauffard, a death solemnly mourned by all the women of the upper Montmartre for three days and nights. In his funeral procession walked crowds larger than those that followed the funeral corteges of the presidents of the Republic, crowds sad and touched to the quick, who raised cries of revenge and abuse against Tom Bill. The bartender, alas, shared very many details but I, unfortunately, paid no attention to them, unaware that later I would become interested in their subject). Tom continued to play his role in all this but with ever-greater resistance, getting bogged down in the sands of daydreams and his growing dissatisfaction.

His memories rearranged the scenery of reality. Beyond the evening, which he spent in his room or on a little walk, opened another evening, taut with the sweetness, stray sounds, stale colors and forgotten smells of his childhood, flies and poverty. Lying with a woman, he grew lost not in love's ecstasy but in whispers reaching him from the courtyard, in the shouts and playful hubbub of children's voices, perhaps seeking in this twittering choir his own voice, perhaps hearing this same sweet, tormenting echo of life from thirty years ago listening in a room where he lay sick and lonely, perhaps hunting the feeble shadows of a paradise lost. Entering a tobacco store, he remembered the treasures he used to find in the cigar boxes, or he would remember the little store where he bought striped sugar pillows. Under the asphalt of the street his soles felt the roughhewn stones of the courtyard on which, as a child, his feet were so often bruised. The maps doubled, streets fell away and sometimes he froze, forgetting himself in the misty rising and falling of memories.

At thirty-six Tom Bill was at the height of his success, he was the scourge of his opponents and women, who liked these spectacles of strength as long as they were not too brutal. But Tom Bill took an account of all this and the results were: bad, despair, hopelessness. The prospects for the future which he had never before considered were agonizingly clear: one more year, a few more years, and he would have to step aside for those younger, just as the older and more seasoned unbeaten opponents had once had to step down for him; then death, death from hunger of a lonely, generally despised wild animal. He could not find even one fact out of the past, not even one moment that he wanted to relive. Therefore it became a self-evident truth, subject to no doubt, that all of his life up to now had been a wasted mistake. And what could this simple and untutored mind, unaware of the arcana and relativism of logistics, think? If the direction of his life had been falser than false, then, this was obvious, only the opposite direction could be right. If strength had deceived him then what could save him if not weakness? What could that heart have felt—the rock-stale bread of a miser-beggar dying of hunger—a heart that was a stranger to the delights and agonies of being divided? It yearned for weakness, as it had formerly yearned for strength.

Perhaps he did not think or feel at all—he knew and he knew without a doubt. To us, miners descending into the deep tunnels of the soul with the double lamp of heart and thought, it is difficult to cut through each stratum when the air is so heavy that our lungs, trained like the lungs of old mares, sound the alarm: stop—death.

Tom Bill decided to be weak. —Was this supposed to come to him with difficulty? Why, he hadn't always been strong, he hadn't always been Tom Bill. The weak, rather frail boy had made himself into a boxer, into a champion of universal fame, by working on himself, with his own stubbornness; his furious, childish anger; and with his desire for revenge. The astounding thing amid the memories in which he was drowning, which separated him from the land of reality, was that there was no memory of the fact that had really determined the direction of his life, the transformation of his biceps, his career, Tom's profession. (A grim scene from a life of squalor, a tragedy common to children living on the city's outskirts: Tom's weak and aging father was beaten up on the street, beaten up badly, cruelly, in Tom's presence—what does it matter if he had been beaten for some vile act committed out of poverty and alcohol. Why go on about this important but very painful sight! I send the reader fond of sadistic descriptions to *The Brothers Karamazov* where he will find an identical scene.)

Tom Bill never mentioned it, yet it was this seemingly trivial fact that shaped his entire life. The desire to avenge the cruel injury he experienced told the six-year-old child to cultivate physical strength, to dream of being an athlete. He attained as much, he could avenge himself. Was he not taking revenge when, stunned by the hardened fist of his opponent, he beat his opponent on the scruff of the neck, on the head, burgeoning muscles and soft flesh, until he was awakened by the warning bells of the judges? He persecuted his opponent as if he had beneath him all the obese and surfeited mugs of the philistines sitting with their wives in the loges—dandies, coquettes, midinettes, students, salesmen, who yearned to taste the atavistic delights of a fight safely, as if he had beneath him the soft, well-fed and bloated mug of the entire globe. But dull with the contempt that these conquered, weak bodies drew from him, Tom Bill's desire for revenge grew smaller until it vanished altogether. Perhaps this is why Tom Bill felt the indifference and emptiness of life? Perhaps this is why he put a minus sign in front of everything that he had experienced until now? And perhaps this is why he yearned for weakness as passionately and violently as he had once longed for strength?

Observation suggested certain facts regarding the victory of weakness over strength. To be weak constituted all the joys of life! Women smiled upon the weak, the weak acquired fortunes, luck was on the side of the weak. He decided to be weak.

But weakness does not come easily. It is difficult to become weak in this world, where even inertia is the torpidity of strength. The inertia of the human soul—habit—which is, and not just according to the Englishman Hume, the heart of being—emphasized and strengthened in the eyes of Tom Bill's opponents the severe contours of his inflated muscles, which he in vain tried to weaken, to eliminate with the effort of his angered will. Comic scenes, worthy of the great Chaplin: the boxer, who while not forgoing professional decency, tries to give in, exposes his weakest side, and the opponent, dumbfounded, distrustful, astounded, suspects a new and dangerous trick in a dangerous and cunning partner, an opponent who not only does not take advantage of these weaknesses but loses himself in conjecture, forgets himself, loses form and becomes an extraordinarily easy victim. If only I were a humorist and could move the reader to tears! The circus public—disoriented and uncertain as to the real intentions and motors of this wrestling match—did not laugh. It would not laugh even if it did know them—it had a separate category for laughter—clowns, and a separate one for wild emotions—the French fight.

Tom Bill had many such victories—victories that were the results of misunderstandings and involuntary. Not many people know how cruel a victory that one does not want can be. But the joyous day came even for Tom Bill: he was defeated. From that day, he surrendered without stopping. The hypnotism of his advantage, of his universal renown was blown to the four winds. Shortly he had to quit the profession altogether.

It seemed to him—or it didn't even seem to him, he was absolutely certain—that the instant he fell, the instant he was beaten, everything would change for the better, completely and forever; the world, so hostile up to now, would turn to him, take him in its arms, embrace him. All this would happen at once and absolutely. How it would happen—he didn't think about; he had a dim feeling, a foretaste of beautiful women, affluence, fatherhood, a quiet but great happiness. All for naught! Instead of smiles, the fangs of hatred and hostility—which had previously been masked by fear—now gleamed openly before him. Instead of happiness, he reaped misery. The world turned to him all right, but only to spit venom in his face.

Tom was not disillusioned—he was dumbfounded. He waited. For the time being he lived on his savings. They did not last long. He had to move from the upper Montmartre to Combat, in the manner of the aging suppliers of prostitution who did not know how to safeguard their old age. He moved into a miserable room, covered with the lichen of dampness and crumbling stone, where his bed barely fit. He lay on it days at a time, or sat on the wall in the courtyard and waited. Not for a miracle—for the luck which is due to each, for any kind of justification for his life. Oh, the stubborn albeit concealed faith in the just logic of destiny! He soon had to get a job in the open markets and train stations.

It is not because of the intervention of the author, fleeting and impatient for a speedy ending, that Tom Bill slipped and fell, one night, while carrying too much weight. The next day he could not get out of bed. In the stubborn provocation of defeat, in the race to death which Tom Bill had himself begun, he had reached the point from which the curve of his fall began to drop at an accelerated rate. Life, to express this sententiously, quickly dispatches a man in whom it has ceased being interested.

Lying alone in his little room, he pursued the scurrying phantoms of his dreams. Doubt came suddenly in the quiet of the night, marked by a pulsating fever. All was lost. His entire life was a failure. Strength had deceived him but weakness had cheated him even more. There was not one moment, not one moment in his entire life, which flew by in his feverish consciousness with crystal clarity, not one moment that he could beckon! He burned with fever and was dying from a blunt hopeless despair. Soon now—death. Death? But for the former champion death was a continuation of life as he knew it, a continuation into infinity, death was temporary life prepared for the consumption of the ages. It never appeared to him as the last reliable respite, he never summoned it, he never longed for, never called on it to cheer him up, a gentle and silent lover, he never bathed in its fluids, in order to flee afterward, when meeting it eye to eye, to fight it off tooth and nail, howl to the heavens with despair, with sorrow and fear. His defeat was absolute and it transcended death, that border where contraband is the only sanctioned form of exchange.

Tom Bill was dying. Suddenly, out of his head burning with despair, bubbled one sentence, one sentence, the straw to which he clung like the proverbial drowning man. A straw is weak, it will not save, but the straw is not important—as long as the dying, unfortunate man has something to cling to. Who threw it out to cheer up the unfortunate Adam? Perhaps it simply arose out of the dirt of fever which spawns rats of nightmares, out of the oils of madness? This one phrase: *Blessed are the weak:* had he really heard it sometime in his childhood, or had he just imagined it? Had he read it, had he really heard it from the revealed book which he did not know, but about which he knew, that it is enough to know that it exists?

If so, if this is what it really said in the revealed book, then not all would be lost. Not for life beyond the grave—he hadn't remembered its existence, he thought about neither heaven nor hell—but for life and death. His defeat would not be so hopeless, his weakness, his life would find the justification his tormented consciousness demanded. If this were really so, he could die calmly. Feeling the hand of death upon him, Tom Bill knew that he was incapable of dying until he knew for sure. That was when he remembered his neighbor.

His neighbor was a Russian, Christ's apostle of mercy, an atheistic St. Francis, a long-haired anarchist with the heart of a dove. The reality of other people wounded him far more than his own. The misery of the world marked him with the stigmata of painful compassion.

But this unbelieving saint was weak. He feared, for example, the agony, the strong sweat of his neighbor; he felt a revulsion in the depths of his subconscious for his neighbor's naked brutal strength. When he met him on the stairs, he wanted to disappear into the wall. Now, hearing his neighbor's violent pounding on the wall and stifling his own trembling, he fought with himself, with his weakness, with his fear, with his revulsion. He was victorious in the struggle with himself, however. Brimming with acquiescence to martyrdom, he went to the athlete who was calling him. The poverty of this agony, the feverish barely comprehensible demand of the dying man to tell him if the Gospels really did mention something about the weak—and if that were so to read it aloud to him—deeply moved the Russian. Returning to get the Gospels, he was overcome by a moment of doubt. The Bible shared a shelf with the works of Nietzsche. He wavered. He, who never lied, had a choice: either a merciful lie or the cruel truth. (Unfortunately, he was wrong. Let us not condemn him, let us try to understand, in order to forgive, for we are better than we really are, than our condemnations and judgments, our instincts and passions, our minds and characters—and in this one thing we see the possibility and divinity of morality.) Knowing Tom as a brutal athlete, the living image of violent and evil strength, the merciful anarchist assumed that it was fear of death, fear of punishment, fear of responsibility, that prompted this muscleman who lived by the truth of the fist to demand a confirmation of God's words that would eternally condemn him. How could he, an apostle of mercy, administer the last cruel blow to this unhappy dying athlete, how could he deprive him of perhaps the last hope, the last joyful doubt; how could he give him this viaticum of severe condemnation as a parting gift? Weighing down his tender conscience with lies, therefore, he decided to give Tom one last comfort. Instead of the Gospels he took Nietzsche and, sitting at the bedside of the strongman—tense with expectation of the words which would finally allow him to permit impatient death to enter—he read aloud not: "Blessed are the weak," but "Blesssed are the strong." In this way, he thought to succor the dying man—still strong not so very long ago—to give him the hope of salvation. He was cruelly mistaken. The sensitive ears of the Russian caught a sound, a feeble sound—neither a moan nor a sigh—through the bitterly tinged, cheerless hard words of the grim philosopher, and his eyes, looking over the page, managed to catch in the half-light of the room the spasmodic relaxation of legs under the plaid blanket and the nervous twitch of cheeks, which sculpts our faces into the statuelike nakedness of humanity: death.

—————

LUCIFER UNEMPLOYED

1

You can't hold the Biblical imagery against him. Looking at the torn clouds on the horizon, he thought: the trampled beard of Jehovah. But high above his head hung a small cloud, flat and motionless like words glued to the vast faded blank of a telegram. Perhaps the message was good because after looking up, the stranger smiled and confidently entered the editorial office of the magazine *Death to the Gods.*

"Here I am to offer you my collaboration," he said to the editor. "I know all the secrets of creation and I will reveal things to you no one else knows."

"Why, that's impossible," the editor replied, "we know everything already. To know everything is our raison d'être. As it is, we have more contributors than subscribers. Maybe some other time."

"But," protested the stranger, "I'm a personal enemy of God!"

"We are not enemies of God. One can't be an enemy of something that doesn't exist. We fight the system that's based on that fiction; we fight tradition, religion, the church . . ."

"I am he who has been fighting the church for centuries! I am Lucifer!" he added in a whisper.

The editor was just about to burst out laughing when the room suddenly shook. Amid the thunder and lightning appeared the same stranger but in another guise, this time as Mephistopheles.

"Perhaps you will recognize me more easily in this rendition? *Ich bin der Geist, der stets verneint!*"

"*Apage Satana!*" shouted the editor, crossing himself franti-
cally. "I believe you are the devil!" he blurted out, barely catching
his breath. "I believe it because you, who are the most stubborn
vestige and perhaps the only being in this universe that really
believes in the existence of God, you come to an antireligious
magazine and propose cooperation! This is exactly the kind of
tactlessness and cheek only a devil would dare exhibit!"

Lucifer left the office so upset that out on the street he tore
a button off his jacket. The button rolled down the sidewalk
pushed along by the wind as if someone were blowing into the
stone horn of the street, luminous at this hour of dusk with the
colors of burnished copper. Lucifer ran after the button, bent
over, and then quickly straightened up and slapped his forehead.
"Guzik!"* he said, "yes, of course, Guzik!"

2

Cleopatra's salon was the place for a rendezvous with The Mysterious. It was here that all the latest metempsychic knowledge
was concentrated, and all the distinguished personalities of spiritism, all the famous media and "better" spirits gathered.
Through the open doors of that salon came and went The
Unknown, looking at its reflection in expensive bronzes, porce-
lains, and mirrors; striking people, raising tables and allowing
itself to be photographed and weighed on subtle, complicated
instruments.

Cleopatra was a former actress with a knack for appealing
to men. These days she was an enthusiastic spiritualist; she
painted herself some rancid color, and kept (from bygone days)

Guzik is the Polish word for "button." Jan Guzik was a famous
medium (immediately following World War I when "spiritism"
was fashionable) whose reputation was somewhat tarnished
when a skeptic flipped on a lightswitch during one of his
seances: the icy hand of the hovering spirit turned out to be
Guzik's cold foot.—TRANS.

a lizardskin album stuffed with reviews, precious stones, superstitions, a book with stage photographs, pension checks, a pseudonym, ribbons from wreaths, a few gestures and the love of Count S. This friendship, which survived traitorous middle age, was the inspiration of poets, who compared it in marvelous elegies to the tender faithfulness of Pyramus and Thisbe.

When Lucifer showed up, almost everyone was there, except for the lady of the house and Count S.: a professor of paleontology, two society lionesses—sitting like two question marks in armchairs—a distinguished lawyer, a fashionable poet, an industrialist, a journalist, and a student. When the chronically late colonel finally arrived, everyone got down to the business of the séance.

Lucifer could just barely remember his neglected skills. All the incantations, signs, magic which once had dazzled the finest of magicians and wizards now slowly issued out of oblivion. He worked hard and conscientiously. When the lights finally came back on, he was tired and hungry. He was led to the dining room, where he revived himself on hors d'oeuvres. After a long wait, Lucifer was called in and the professor of paleontology broke the solemn silence of those gathered:

"You really did perform rather unusual feats. A magician or miracle worker, you conjured up an array of shapes and colors that the eye could not encompass, nor memory retain. We saw things so mysterious that only distant allegories allowed us to understand their forms. We saw spiraling specters among wandering mirrored surfaces and prisms. We saw clouds, which night transforms into diamonds, burning on the coals of heaven. We saw pools of water spurting bouquets of crystal shapes, birds which spoke like humans—each word blossoming into a rose bush. We saw angels with gleaming wings and with wings as transparent as a fly's. We saw angel-cowboys, hunting scattered herds of half-people, half-animals. We saw oceans covered with fish scales. We saw a woman with hair like a nest of snakes, the one whom antiquity called Medusa, and her face was mild and sweet beyond expression. We saw an enormous tree, whose tip one could not see but in whose galactic branches swayed a nest, the earth. We saw purple grottoes full of colored shade. From here flowed an enormous river that branched into four arms like a swastika. We saw the land which Genesis calls Hewilath, where gold blooms and one can find bdellium and onychin. Among the lushness of foliage we found two bare trees, and a hiss from beneath the tall singing grasses told us that this was the tree of life and the tree of the knowledge of good and evil. We moved slowly and solemnly, for the air was full of demons, and their nature was as delicate and frail as a soap bubble. Strange substances swarmed around us, black as coal and as colorful as Oceanids. We saw wandering clods of earth shouting amen, rocks proclaiming glory on high, singing streams. We saw all this and much more.

"But our instruments, our very precise, very sensitive, very scientific instruments confirmed not a trace of metaplasm. We will not judge your feats—charlatanism, poetry, or miracle—that's none of our business, we are the representatives of a new science, whose aim is the thorough study of the unknown properties of metaplasm. However wondrous your works, you and your ilk are a detriment to our cause by exploiting our young movement, discrediting it in the opinion of serious society. We have decided to warn all metapsychic societies against you."

Lightning bolts, the angry signatures of God, streaked across a sky swollen with clouds. Since the devil does not know how to sleep, Lucifer wandered along the sidestreets, stopping at dives where the ruddy Slavic accordion had not yet given way to the mystical black man of the jazz band.

3

"Modern times," said Lucifer the next day, walking into the workshop of a famous inventor, "belong to technicians. Edison is the Merlin of the twentieth century. What can a poor devil become in these times if not an inventor?"

"I know," replied the inventor, as Lucifer boasted of some of the feats he had performed in the past. "I heard something about them, about how you transported old women through the air on brooms, for instance, but I never heard that you could transport a hundred passengers across the Atlantic, swathing them in luxury and comfort. I read, too, that you made beautiful women appear to crazed hermits in Egyptian deserts, but I did not read that you could produce dramatic apparitions before a million people, daily, all over the world! You were also mentioned in connection with the fish Leviathan, but no one mentioned the speeding belly of the 'Leviathan'—in whose interior thousands devote themselves to life's pleasures, dancing and champagne— that parts the seas. Your miracles were haphazard, ours are organized, permanent, and utilitarian. Our civilization is a miracle introduced into the system. Our civilization is a system of miracles. And who today would call on you to do miracles when the advertisements on Fifth Avenue and the lights of the elevator in the Eiffel Tower have changed night into day with a luminosity a hundred times more magnificent than that borne by Lucifer?"

4

"But there was a time when the human race adored me. The Middle Ages honored me and saw me everywhere: in beautiful old gods, in yellowed parchment flowering with wisdom, in the purple of a rose, in the beauty of a woman's body, in love, in the song of the nightingale. I remember well (a certain German poet reminded me of this) those pious doctors, wandering along wooded trails and discoursing on: the dual holiness of the Mother of God? the seven virtues of pigeons? who would suddenly stop before a rose bush from which came the trilling of a nightingale. 'That's probably an evil spirit, the tempter,' one of the theologians would say. 'Yes, I am an evil spirit,' answered the nightingale and laughed. The next day the theologians expired. That's the kind of thing that went on in the thick of the Middle Ages. And even though some master, overly tormented by his body, would imagine me in hideous chimerical forms, even though a pious canon would occasionally throw his chamber pot and cover me with stinking sop, everything that was beautiful bore my name. I was entreated for wisdom, power, youth, gold. Stakes and the minds of demonologists burned in my glory. After all it was I who brought pestilence and disease and it was I who healed the infirm. And although I am not sure if I was Zalmoxis, that mythical teacher of Aesculapius," said Lucifer passing a pharmacy, "to this day you can see my symbol on the shield of shrines of medicine, the image of the serpent, the beast whose form I took when getting to know humanity. Medicine is my faithful servant to this day."

"Medicine is a science," said the president of the Chamber of Medicine, "which examines the state called illness. The fact that medicine heals and kills people, well, that is less important, resulting from the properties of medicine as an experimental science. For you see, ever since new scientific theories revealed that illness is a normal and desired state, medicine is less and less the science of healing. Therapy without diagnosis is not medicine, it's quackery which has stopped amusing even the snobs. Medicine has ceased being the domain of the devil; it has broken the umbilical cord binding Lucifer to pathology. Where people once saw the devil, they now see the all-too-powerful attributes of sex. That which you used to do is now done better and more simply. Today Faust calls not you but Steinach. Diseases which you once cured have now disappeared altogether or have become so common that they have quit being illnesses. Leprosy, for example, is becoming extinct; madness is no longer considered an illness. Take a look at men and women everywhere when they gather to have a good time. You will see them possessed by gyrations that would have been impossible to see even in the heyday of witches' sabbaths. Ask them if they want to be cured!"

It's true, thought Lucifer, Witches' Hill now boasts polished floors and floodlights. The gyrations, which someone has called the dance of the sullen heads and joyous genitalia, are heroic injections of prostitution whereby the bourgeoisie tries to resuscitate the lifeless body of the family. The old mode of sexual selection, which was faced with extinction, now extends its millions of arms to women's bodies. Nevertheless, this is just one of the specters of modern times. No matter how red with blood, how green with nihilism, how violet with perversion, it all adds up to an incredible, fairy-tale whiteness. That whiteness is work, production, industrialization! The scales, on which a wanton, diamond-studded Europa is dancing, are balanced with coal. And coal *wins*. The interests of oil trusts guide the pencils of diplomats who trace the map of the world. Today oil is the blood of society.

"I can draw new sources of crude from any spot that I strike with my hoo— I mean heel," said Lucifer to the General Secretary of The Oil Company.

"New oil wells!" shouted the Secretary, horrified. "Heaven forbid! There is too much oil as there is. New wells: that would mean a drop in prices, bankruptcy, unemployment, depression, communism! American exporters are dumping wheat so that prices don't drop. There's too much wheat, oil, coal; there's too much of everything, and those are only the inferior additives to the real values which man has created: prices, turnover, the Stock Exchange."

5

Lucifer spoke to the king of the Stock Exchange, a thin, wizened old man whose face reminded him of ancient copper masks. The green and brown spots on his cheeks heightened the similarity. Lucifer told him of the golden calf, the cult of Mammon, about the desire for riches and pleasure he had once aroused in people. The old man heard him out and said:

"The language of brute materialism which you use is alien to me. We are spiritualists, proclaimers of ideas, zealous apostles of idealism. We are the puritans of a new morality, the simplified mathematical morality of supply and demand, buying and selling. We are ascetics, knights renouncing material goods, kings of poverty. The great Stinnes wore one and the same suit for fifteen years: longer than Isabella Castile wore her undergarments. I myself live on only fruit, milk, vegetables, and chocolate. We are the impoverished guardians of treasures, rulers of riches. We are the organizers of chaos. Our kingdom is not concrete and not material. Our might, our essence—the check—is an abstraction, a number, a symbol. It is an order, a command. It is by this command that we bankrupt or make rich, by this order that we destroy or create. With it we herd the masses of workers into factories, with it we turn their muscles and nerves into the steel that may later be used to murder them. It is this command that hisses in the retort of the investor, pushes the pen of the inspired poet, strangles Angersteins with its fingers, puffs up the cheeks of the black player in the jazz band, transforms the scraps of skin from Denke's victims into shoelaces, twists into hatred the lips of the people's tribune, sways the hips of streetwalkers, sings Salvation Army hymns, cries out with the first cry of the newborn and gasps with the last breath of the dying. It is by fiat that we build and fill mortuaries, temples, houses of prostitution, universities, factories, hotels, palaces, ships, skyscrapers, planes, hospitals. It determines the borders of countries, declares wars, controls the number of births and the percentage of deaths and suicides. This is not your golden calf, this is not luxury or pleasure—this is the stern *principle* of gold, luxury and pleasure. Real gold, our gold, is power, virtue, it is the virtue of virtues, it is the *idea*! We are ascetics laden with responsibility for running the world. The stock market is our temple of idealism, the temple of God, the great, almighty ruler, Jehovah! Now," he added with a smile, "you understand why there are so many of the Chosen People here."

Oh well, mercantilism doesn't suit my nature anyway, thought the devil, leaving the king of the Stock Exchange. I haven't the knack for commercial dealings. I'm too gullible and too easy to cheat. I used to pay the highest prices for the most mediocre souls, and then when it came to collecting, they'd slip through my fingers by reciting some cheap prayer! And there isn't even a court that a poor devil could turn to for justice!

6

"If Nurmi* had broken a leg, it certainly would have caused a greater uproar than if Cleopatra had lost her nose in her day. If Dempsey's arm had been amputated, what would have happened to the pride of the United States? Sport is the banner of modern times. Not many years ago, sport was the oddity of esoteric clubs. Today it is a force, a religion which unites people from one pole to the other in a procession of victory. Sport is the religion of the flesh and I was always its most zealous and persecuted apostle."

"That is true," said the president of the sports club, "and what's more, the first sporting event was your work. I have in mind the so-called fall of the angels, a record leap from heaven, after which people say you contracted a limp in one leg. Sport is the form of today's world. A team's colors are far more important than racial colors. In an age of democracy, pacificism, and pan-Europeanism, sports are the only rational ground on which patriotism can express itself in humanitarian competition between people and classes. The workers' team defends the sanctity of its crest against that of the bourgeois team, and the goal made by the workers' team rips apart the net of capitalism far more effectively than a terrorist bomb. Nurmi's legs covered poor, rocky Finland with fame, and Dempsey's fist brought

*Paavo Nurmi, "the Flying Finn," won four gold medals in the Summer Olympic Games of 1924—TRANS.

France down better than the heavy columns of its debt to America. Carpentier's fall echoed more loudly than the fall of the National Assembly, and Gallic gods cried over him in their forest thickets. Who, except for adventurers, poets, geographers, and stamp collectors, ever knew anything about Uruguay? Today Uruguay is sacred, universally worshipped! Today the world bows before Uruguay's flags. And the day is not far off when battles for power, dogma, bread, will take place not on bloody battlefields and barricades but on sunny playgrounds, arenas, stadiums . . . Even so, how could I connect Lucifer with sports? The spirit of sports is the spirit of true democracy, the spirit of free competition, where training, endurance, skill, and the system of mechanical properties of the body are the victors. You, on the other hand, who possess wonderworking capabilities, have an incalculable, metaphysical, and incorporeal advantage over your opponents from the start."

"My miracles are child's play next to the organized miracles of civilization," said Lucifer. "Besides, my miracles are illusory. That, at least, is what St. Thomas Aquinas claims in his *Summa Theologica* 1 *quaestio* 110-14, *ad* 2, and he is an authority I would not dare contradict!"

7

Startled by horns and having jumped away from the caravans of cars (Little Brother Car, St. Francis would have said), Lucifer stood on the island in the middle of the square, next to a policeman who was directing the movement of countless vehicles.

Behold the conductor of the noisy orchestration of the city, thought Lucifer, behold Moses, who with his little baton stops the automotive idols and who with his little baton floods the passages with them again.

"I am Moses," said the policeman. "I am the tablets of the Ten Commandments. I am the personification of the code of law. I am the measure of all things. I am an island of truth in oceans of lawlessness. For no one is without fault in the eyes of a policeman—who is law, who is the measure of all things. I imprison some people in brick cages, others in the prisons of city streets. I stand at the intersection and watch: no one can get away from me. This morning I saw a god running away from me with a bomb in his pocket. He was running away from me but he did not get away. There is no perfection on earth! Unfortunately! I too am a man, I too am a trespasser, and I keep an eye on myself. No one is without fault in the eyes of a policeman who is law, who keeps guard, looks, pursues and watches over."*

8

Across from the policeman was a den of anarchy. The policeman kept an eye on it, but often, overcome by revulsion, he turned his back on its poisonous fumes. Lucifer went in because it was a poet's café and this time Lucifer had decided to become a poet.

Poets and snobs congregated here: poets and snobbery go together as nicely as a thrown rock and ripples in water. This was the place where the wisemen who sucked wisdom out of the pacifier of words got together. What a shame! What a shame that for so long we have lacked a nurse of revelation! Words are tubercular, syphilitic, and preserve in their countless tissues swarming colonies of ambiguous microbes. By means of the same words some pave the way for European Buddhism, others propagate Orthodoxy and Catholicism. The latter are blood brothers to the inventors of deadly dynamite, all, of course, in the name of pacifism. And even if one finds healthy words in some out-of-the-way place, words securely fastened to the earth, even then poets would unchain them and punch them into the empty,

*We all know that Lucifer should not have believed the beautiful words of the policeman. We know that the police are not only the organizers but, above all, a first-rate organization of crime and lawlessness.

vacant sky. What a shame! What a shame! And it's not as if they were mad dogs. They were only the colored bubbles of words.

In the café Lucifer came across the representatives of two very different poetic camps. The first one was made up of carefree Don Juans and Lancelots of inspiration, the blind worshippers of the holiness of talent and the poetic medium. They gave themselves passively to the fluids of a temporal lyricism, which visited and flowed through them without interference. They celebrated trees, love, death, all that is immutable from the beginning of creation. The second group, on the other hand, worshipped anything that was new, they desired to encompass the present moment, to grasp its multilayered rhythm. The first group recognized the meaning of feeling, the second the feeling of meaning. They tried to overcome the chasm between the multiplicity and the changeability of material and mental life, and the limitations of a completely exhausted emotionalism. Some of them acomplished this by flying blindly on the delicate apparatus of trickery; others with a breakneck *salto mortale* of inner contradictions; others, raving like madmen, sought miracles; a few burrowed tunnels into the subconscious. Others worshipped modern times, the proletariat and machines, treating them the way Negro *élégants* treated the pants they flung over their shoulders.

"You reek of metaphysics," said a representative of this group, "your breath has the odor of a moldering bookshop, and your face is the face of a merchant of ancient culture: it is dripping with cosmic melancholy. These are the things we hate most of all."

"You are too comprehensible," pronounced the other type, "to be a real poet. We have entered a stage in our civilization where, as a result of overwhelming specialization, every real bit of progress in one field sets the individual back in all others. And so a good physicist or doctor cannot help being an ignoramus in matters of poetry. This is the real reason for incomprehensibility, which can only become more pervasive. Poets, that is, real poets, in a few years will all either be locked up in hospitals as professional madmen, or they will win for poetry the same right to specialization as mathematics, for example, which, except for a few elementary areas, is accessible only to specialists."

Taking his leave rather coolly, Lucifer sat down at the table of the opposing group.

"There is neither new nor old poetry," proclaimed their leader. "There has always been and always will be only good or bad poetry. Good poetry is talent. Talent is a gift from God; therefore, you cannot possess it. Words are like trees. Let us watch so that the enemy—the evil spirit, the serpent—tempter!—does not sneak in between their branches. But then," he added, "maybe I'm just talking nonsense."

Another was more blunt. "You have no talent," he said. "Proof? My word of honor."

"I knew a poet," said a friend of the poets to Lucifer (this friend of the poets was an unproductive thinker, whose head was a veritable hotel of ideas never registered, a hotel rented for hours of ecstasy and cynicism), "who sought inspiration in water closets. Whenever he had nothing to write about or whenever he lost his train of thought in a poem, he would go to a water closet and sit there until he found his lost Muse. Once when he was working on a masterpiece, he tripped on a missing word. So he locked himself in a toilet and waited for the return of the fugitive. Who knows what invocations he used during those long hours of yearning? When his friends kicked in the doors, they found an emaciated half-corpse which had to be delivered to an insane asylum. What has happened to poetry? Has it abandoned its last chapel, or does it return occasionally and scare the poor radio amateur, who has moved into the apartment of the poet? At any rate, some people assure us that it is possible to come across poetry in the cheapest public houses on the outskirts of town, where inhaling the stinking fumes, it dreams about *odor sanctitatis* whose secret is still unknown to Guerlain or Coty. I also know poets, unhappy Midases choking on the gold of their images, who suffer all the more because no one believes in the reality of that gold. These are always the invalids of an antiquated way of getting to know the world. Yes, yes, there are fewer and fewer poets, but more and more amateur radio buffs."

In front of the café, a crowd of people was looking at a carriage with a broken axle, which a potbellied driver was trying to fix, cursing aloud and swearing that tomorrow he would become a taxi driver.

If, thought Lucifer, the broken axle of that cab, which will end up in the junkyard tomorrow, could be considered the axle of the world, we would have an accurate picture of these people.

Lucifer had acquired this penchant for metaphor from his adversary.

9

"He who warned people against the spirit of history is long dead. History made quite a dupe of him for one thing. When he cursed her, she turned her backside to him. He, not recognizing history, adored that backside, for he adored the future, which is the backside of the past. We see her face only when she is behind us. Nietzsche died, but history is still the mistress of life. She nourishes the proletarian infant with revenge and feeds monkey serum to the aging bourgeoisie. Who could be a better historian than I?"

Lucifer was telling a well-known historian: "Balaam's ass talked because it was equipped with a kind of record player. It was a pretty primitive model, of course, and as for King David's counting of the Jews, which according to the Book of Paralipomenon was done at my bidding and according to the Book of Kings was done at the bidding of the Lord God, well, the true version is the latter. This is not the first time that they are saddling me with the sins of my opponent. I am, unfortunately, a scapegoat upon whom are heaped all the flaws of the world and its creator. Apropos, I am afraid (I am not familiar with the most recent biblical literature) that some learned metaphysician, basing his conclusion on the above-mentioned contradiction, will identify me with God. I am terribly afraid of this because I am an Individualist, an egotist, and I am very attached to my separate identity. I don't like to strut about in borrowed plumes. From this you may judge for yourself what a liar Tertullian was when he called me an ape of God. Equally far from the truth is anyone who considers the world a mirror in front of which I learn to ape God. But enough of these digressions. Getting back to the subject, I can tell you where Paradise was. Or I can give you pretty accurate information about the ten lost tribes of Israel. I have no doubt that you will also want to hear, out of curiosity, about the architectural flaw in the structure of the Tower of Babel."

"You will excuse me," exclaimed the scholar, but this does not interest me in the least. History has nothing to do with your stories."

"What?!!" answered Lucifer, enraged. "But this is the *truth*!!"

"Truth? What truth? If you have in mind what was once called 'historical truth,' factual, absolute truth, then that truth no longer exists. The relativity of events, the elementary ambiguity of historical experiences, dependent on this, that or some other selection of facts and interpretations, have long discouraged historians from seeking such truth. Today historical truth is nothing but a formal truth. History, revived by methods borrowed from mathematics, is made up of systems which order experience and which are more or less appropriate to it and express it in various conceptual configurations. Just as in the example that every given length, multiplied by a whole number, sufficiently great, will be greater than any other length, however great, is true or false—depending on whether or not one accepts the Archimedean system of geometry or a geometric system that is non-Archimedean—so, too, is it with a given historical law. Even a fact is true or false depending on which system one accepts: historical materialism, idealism, or any of the many other possible systems. But in talking to you I am wasting my time, which I put to far better use for humanity when I work on my four-volume study of the economic reasons for the development and decline of the city of Gletau."

10

"Journalism is my element," Lucifer was saying to a well-known journalist. "That famous exchange with Job was nothing but a journalist's interview. One could say practically the same thing for almost all of the temptations of saints."

"I don't know if temptation was a journalistic interview at a time when there were no newspapers, but one thing is sure: the human race cannot live without religion, faith, a church. Faith is eternal. Only its object changes. First there is faith in nature, then in idols; next there's faith in tradition, in the spoken word; today there is faith in the printed word. Gutenberg's primitive printing press was the modern man's stable of Bethlehem. The book is the religion of individuals, the newspaper is the religion of the masses. Faith is eternally the same; only its object changes. Today the sanctuary of faith is the press. Do not the faithful of this church read the morning paper every morning and the evening paper every evening, just as they had once said their morning and evening prayers? There was a time when a sure indication of faith was the miracle. People admired the prophet who predicted storms and saw through walls—today one reads meteorological prognostications; and people admire the boy whose eyes were x-rayed by lightning, allowing him to penetrate walls with his vision. It is true that one page of the newspaper contains more descriptions of miracles than there are in the entire Bible. But it is not the miracle which spawns faith but the reverse. Faith in the press is the faith of the twentieth century. The power of its suggestion is inexpressible. Like all religions, it describes the position of the individual in the universe. Like every religion, it is the rock upon which rests the state. Who really cares about politics, military conflicts in distant countries, skirmishes, pacts, armies, except for a small number of directly involved individuals? It is the press that has infected the human race with an artificial interest in these issues; if it were not for the press, they would vanish without a trace because nobody would be interested. So what could we, the victorious church, the church triumphant, possibly have in common with the eternal rebel of the church? Let us add that we are polytheists. You, on the other hand, are a monotheist. But what is more important: people say that ever since Martin Luther threw an inkpot at you, you hate ink, and you reputedly hate printer's ink most of all."

11

Lucifer is talking to the Minister of War who has received him on behalf of the Cabinet Chief.

"I am the principal of war and diplomacy. I am the ruler of deception and betrayal. I am the spirit of intrigue and plotting. My role from time immemorial has been to turn people against one another. There is nothing left for me to do except become a diplomat."

"What!" shouted the outraged minister. "How so? You mean the world has become an impoverished slaughterhouse where the human race has lost ten million of the flower of its youth, and deprived seven million of eyes, hands, and legs, in order to return to its old prewar methods of intrigue, plotting and secret diplomacy! No Sir! Today we know methods a hundred times more sophisticated and intimidating which are called: openness, frankness, conferences, plebiscites, arbitration! We, the Ministers of War of fifty-four countries, belong to the League of Nations and are honorary presidents of pacifist societies. We have created a new peace, a peace which is continual war, war carried on coolly, cautiously, clearly, openly, democratically. Let Europe sleep, let that poor old wheezing mare slumber on! Let her dream that she is a thoroughbred running a heavy obstacle course. Let Europe sleep; we are keeping watch for her! We are arming ourselves, we are building bomb factories, we are stockpiling submarines, zeppelins, poison gas, tanks, death rays, cruisers, cannons, bombs, grenades. Let Europe, that exhausted old mare, doze on! Let her dream her cozy dream about peace—

we, the Ministers of War, will awaken her at the appropriate moment. But by then she will be nothing but a bloody, brainless pulp in the bleeding wound of the world."

12

When Lucifer reappeared on the street, invisible artillery from behind the trench of the horizon was shooting tiny stars all over the heavens. Lucifer was sad and downcast. He wandered about the city, fearing the awful indifference of the people around him. He mingled with the densest crowds, rubbed up against passersby, but nothing helped: he felt lonelier here than amid the interplanetary spaces. The glare of advertisements and the cold light of window displays and film theaters washed over him like an icy rain. After a few hours of aimless wandering in the streets, his craving for company was so strong and persistent that, even though he didn't smoke, he bought a pack of cigarettes from a street vendor just to have someone to talk to. Luckily the vendor—an extremely frail, small man, in his twenties, with very ugly, obviously Semitic features—was talkative and told Lucifer about his wanderings all over Europe. He had escaped conscription by fleeing abroad: in Berlin he worked in a cigarette factory; in Paris he sold newspapers and cocaine; in Brussels, vacuum cleaners; in Barcelona, oranges; in Switzerland, wristwatches.

"Go to Australia, America," he said as they parted. "You won't be able to vent your energy here in Europe."

Lucifer laughed. The contrast between the words and the frail, sickly figure of the salesman was so outrageous that he regained his sense of humor. He decided to go to a restaurant that was alluring even at a distance because of its loud music and warm animal odor of meat. He was happy to discover that all of the tables were occupied. He had to share a table. Lucifer immediately spotted someone sitting alone. The man was about forty years old and his twitching face (with yellow and green blots the color of moss-covered tree bark) betrayed an intellectual and a man with a heart condition. The stranger was equally happy to have company, but for a few minutes there was an awkward silence, extinguished by the jazz band. On the table top Lucifer read a poem which the stranger had probably just written.

> Clouds sang out in chorus, in the glories of God's
> twilight,
> On bottom the blue clouds, on top those of red
> light.
>
> He whiffed up his nose the smell of salty breeze,
> Which in the cracks of maps for years lay under
> key.
>
> When the clouds were stifled, the hot winds died
> away,
> Anti-Christ upon the cross was stretched and
> nailed to stay.
>
> "Lucifer! Lucifer!"—but there came no echo
> And his hands dropped, helpless, like a Polish
> weeping willow.
>
> By nightfall exorcisms bloomed in starry clusters,
> The musky scent of clouds losing all their muster.
>
> But what can the night do to help the crucified?
> Again the sword pierced him; divine drink fled his
> side—
>
> (He who at the wedding changed water into wine,
> From wine inside his blood, he summons milksop
> brine)
>
> Blood became a blue stream, of graceful ordered
> calm,
> Which frenzied women catch up in their lips and
> palms,
>
> Flows over, and roots up, rose goblets, human
> hearts,
> On which shrubs, fish and bird are etched in
> ancient art.

> Heat from out the'hot night, the squalls of sighs
>   and moans—
> Well-heard, afflicted gnashing teeth—wails and
>   then groans!
>
> Old bogeys through this mass of blackened, horrid
>   sound,
> We come back from the sea, once hurled there to
>   drown.
>
> And should the bloodred knife of day assault our
>   heads,
> Our snouts we'll keep burrowed safe in the hot
>   sand beds.

"A beautiful poem," said Lucifer, "so metaphysical. There is less and less of that these days. Driven out by science, metaphysics is leaving our sad planet."

"On the contrary, the development of science means the renaissance or rather the appearance of a real metaphysics."

"What a paradox."

"Not in the least. One should recognize the real limits and object of metaphysics. My theory allows for an easy distinction between metaphysics and science, giving each a different raison d'être. Metaphysics is an individual interpretation of the collective consciousness, that is, science. Science, as such, is always the product of a collectivity, not of the individual. Science requires tradition; one of its more important criteria is its universality. Here the collective consciousness, whose organ is science, does not want and is not able to occupy itself with problems concerning the essence of Being, etc. In general, the interpretation of relationships alone makes up its rightful subject. The aim of science is to give a picture of the world as a system of equations, which in closest approximation correspond to empirical reality. The interpretation of these equations is the task of metaphysics, the task of those elements of the individual consciousness which do not enter into the area of collective consciousness, but which I would label, rather unhappily, intranscendental. Whether or not there is a limited or unlimited amount of these types of metaphysical systems—that is a question I cannot yet answer. So the development of science is followed by the development of its interpretation, that is, metaphysics. There was a time when religion brought about the development of science in a similar way. For religion is nothing other than the construction of a collectivity based on individual consciousness. Welding individual consciousnesses into a collectivity brought about the creation of the only collective consciousness that was commensurate with the external world."

"What blasphemy!" shouted Lucifer, who had repeatedly tried to interrupt. "What a shameless degrading of metaphysics to the role of individual interpretation, reducing it to the personal affairs of the individual! Metaphysics which lives, which is an active and driving force, which is sitting right across from you and conversing with you! And with what truly modern, cynical ease you relegate metaphysics to this subordinate, meager and comic existence."

"Cynical ease? An illusion. You will not believe how many years I have suffered, how many feverish nights I have spent trying to subdue this turbulent enormity of feelings, impressions, and thoughts into some kind of picture of the world, to fuse them into a whole. There is not a thought or belief of which I have not been first an ardent apostle and then an ardent apostate. The ease and simplicity of which you accuse me are merely the results of an attained reward, the highest which man is capable of receiving: an active joyous peace. This peace is the blissful attainment of every man who has worked out a productive Weltanschauung. Mine is all the more certain in that it is buttressed by relativity. A productive Weltanschauung is a talisman, a magic coin which—no matter how often you spend it—will always be in your pocket."

"O what malicious and bitter irony! All talismans are deceptions. I know all about this because I am their creator and counterfeiter. As for *your* coin, I advise you not to spend it if you do not want to risk disillusionment and danger. I am proof, living, viable proof of the error of your Weltanschauung; obvious, palpable proof which destroys any relativity. I—I am Lucifer!"

Long after midnight, the two left the restaurant and went their separate ways. Lucifer had barely gone a few steps when he heard a gunshot. He turned around. Flower vendors, convivial women, and belated libertines were running towards the restaurant from everywhere. On the sidewalk lay the stranger, his face covered with blood. The cigarette vendor was bending over him. Lucifer raised the collar of his coat and walked away as quickly as he could.

13

"I am very sorry," said the director of the circus, an overweight gentleman with the face of a friendly animal, "today I sent away my last clown. Ah, today's public acknowledges neither clowns nor acrobats, neither jugglers, nor magicians, not even bareback riders, those gorgeous butterflies fused to horse torsos! Today you have to give them machines, motorcycles, technology. Unfortunately, real art is dying because of the exhaustion of the metaphysical instinct via the mechanization of society. I myself am an artist at heart, but what can I do: such are the times."

14

"But there was a time when I had so many zealous apostles! They summoned me with various names, those ecstatic blasphemers, heresiarchs, epileptic high priest-renegades, celebrating black masses on the bellies of women, as the French writer Huysmans so beautifully describes. I'll round them up and rebuild my church on earth."

After a long search he found out that the majority of them had died. Some were directors of banks and went to church on Sundays with their families. Others had simply been converted. There was a story about one, however, who had apparently remained true to his beliefs. Lucifer found him in the basement of a gigantic department store. The only furnishing in the room was a moldering mattress with an equally decrepit old man lying on it. The mattress and old man mimicked each other. Lucifer let him know who he was in a dazzling speech, in a marvelous display of seductive eloquence. All for naught. The old man was deaf, dumb, and blind, and Lucifer could not find out if he— Lucifer's last living disciple—had remained true to his master, or whether, out of fright, the old man had renounced him for all eternity.

15

In my youth I was far more cunning, thought Satan; I knew that one had to attack from the weak side. I worked through woman, who always wants to be tempted. A woman has good intentions and a wicked nature. Satan, on the other hand, has the reverse, according to Saint Thomas, that is, a good nature and evil intentions. Actually it is not man and woman that make a complementary pair; it is woman and the devil.

Miss Circe, a well known showgirl from the music hall, said, "Eve, our ancient mother, was tempted by the devil, because he appeared in the form of a serpent. If he had appeared in the form of a man, she probably would not have been tempted, but he certainly would have been converted. We became victims of our own gullibility. Since that time we have been in the vanguard of our master's armies (and what were we to do once men began turning our natural parts into the gates of Hell? We knew how to draw more pleasure from them than a poet could draw from his inkpot). From that day on we kissed the smelly rear ends of goats and smeared ourselves with a disgusting salve made of priest's excrement, liver of a newborn babe, blood of a toad, belladonna, and wormwood. We gave ourselves to Satan in spite of terrible pain because giving ourselves to this creature (who, having no seed of his own, fertilized us with the sperm taken from our relations with men) was in keeping with our sexual complexes, our desire for perversion. Today, though, we have lesbian love, combined with the love of men in all possible forms. Today you can see a goat on rue Chabannais for twenty-five francs. It's too bad but everything has gotten cheap, and the strong old gods have died. Today we study Freud and worry that we slough our maidenhood in vain by giving ourselves to the phallus. Today we work like men or wear our hair like men. Today we run away from the knowledge of good and evil. Today a woman goes to the music hall the way she once went to a convent. We are, nevertheless, mere mortals. We die in love as we do in death. . . . Today, you gorgeous male, we just want to get even! Since Lucifer tempted a woman, it is only right that a woman should convert him."

16

Lucifer had no choice. All roads turned out to be closed and so led indirectly to Rome. Miss Circe was converting Lucifer. One day she decided the sinner was sufficiently penitent and she drove him to the bishop, a man known for his erudition and piety. She waited for Lucifer in her luxurious Hispano-Suiza.

"I have sinned grievously," said Lucifer to the bishop. "I talked Adam into sinning out of my own envy and pride."

The bishop raised his eyes to the heavens and cried out in ecstasy:

> O certe necessarium Adae peccatum,
> Quod Christi morte deletum est.
> O felix culpa, quae talem ac tantum
> Meruit habere Redemptorem.*

*O most necessssary sin of Adam/Which was washed away by the death of Christ./O blissful guilt which merits such a Redeemer.

"Forgive me," said Lucifer, "but my Latin is rusty and I do not understand Your Holiness's words. I am Lucifer. The Church and I have been Siamese twins. Did not one of the popes say that if Satan did not exist, we would have to invent him? I was the Siamese twin of holiness, grown together with it at the sex organs. We were Siamese brothers—I and the Church. But today I am only its humblest servant. I have come to humble myself."

The bishop blessed and prostrated himself:

"O my Savior, you have visited a most difficult trial upon me. I am weak and old with the false purity of my white hair. O my Lord, I have fought the devil all of my life, and my heart has grown hard against the temptations of sin, but today, O God, when you send him to me converted, today I am weaker than ever, my heart has softened and is fluttering like a bird. My God, the night is dark around me, as dark as my soul which I cannot comprehend. O Savior, give me a sign, tell me what I should do, for I am old and weak and easily given to sin. And lead us not into temptation. But deliver us from evil. Amen."

The bishop spent a long time in prayer. Finally, he got up and, not looking at Lucifer, told him to come again in three days. During that time the bishop fasted and prayed. On the morning of the third day he fell asleep and, lo, he had a prophetic dream. But he couldn't remember it when he got up.

That evening the devil returned.

"My son," said the bishop, "I have to choose between sinning by not accepting your conversion and sinning by accepting it. To accept it, I would have to believe that the devil can be converted, which is what Origen once taught, but which was severely condemned by the Church. I would thereby commit the sin of heresy!—a sin which I fear above all else. So I will do better to take on only the sin of not accepting your conversion, which is all the more impossible since, even according to Origen's heresy, your conversion is supposed to take place on the *last* day. And I have not seen the fifteen signs which are supposed to precede it. And could I"—he added after a moment—"be the hand that sets fire to the Holy Church that I love more than life itself? I know that the Church, whose founding principle is the struggle with the devil, would cease to exist if the devil were converted."

After Lucifer left, the bishop whispered to himself, "Why didn't I let him in on the secret of the Catholic Church: that God and the devil have long been reconciled by their common opponent—humanity?" The bishop fell into an armchair and wept bitterly.

After finding out that Original Sin could not be redeemed through Lucifer, Miss Circe, who had been waiting for Lucifer in the car, quarreled with him and drove off alone. Lucifer later heard she had become the mistress of a Russian prince, a paid dancer from the rue Pigalle, and of a certain Mr. Scott, a canned goods manufacturer from Chicago.

17

What is my heart that it did not die of pleasure that night? In the morning, on the street, I saw the sun on the outstretched palm of dawn. Its blazing light fell on the chunky café owner who was sluggishly opening his establishment. He was surprised to find a client (unusual at this hour), shivering and huddled in the morning cold, waiting to enter the dark café. The owner wanted to say something but was unable to think of anything and so went about his usual work. The guest hid himself in the corner of an adjoining room. Around him chairs were piled one on top of the other as if they wanted to penetrate the unknown pleasure of sitting. The stranger ordered a glass of milk. A sleepy-faced waiter brought it quickly and returned to the counter. The stranger remained in the room alone. He looked the room over, carefully pulled out his revolver and put the barrel to his temple.

"*Attendez!*" boomed a voice and a hand tore the pistol away.

The desperate stranger opened his eyes with some difficulty. Before him stood someone whose face was obscured by the semidarkness. He was immobile, but it seemed to the stranger

that he vibrated with imperceptible movement, and that he possessed not two pairs but bunches of trembling appendages.

The stranger was dumbfounded. He had looked around the
room earlier—there had been no one in it. With the intervention
came something miraculous, unexpected, fantastic.

"Who are you, what do you want?" he asked in a hoarse
whisper.

"I am interested in suicides. I am a journalist. I gather sta-
tistics and am writing a book about suicides among people and
scorpions. I examine suicide from a biological, economic, psychological, and philosophical standpoint. I merely want some
information from you after which you can resume your activity."

"You can find my story in the works of many authors, whose
names I do not remember. I remember only a two-volume work
by one Roscoff, published in Leipzig in 1869. I am the devil. I
am an unemployed devil, and that is the reason for the suicide
that I am about to commit. The modern world doesn't need me.
It is cleansed of all that is demonic. I am a superfluous man (I
probably deserve that title, at least the title of man *honoris
causa*). The world is *plus diabolique que le diable même*. No, not
even that. It is an infernal cocktail, in which God himself cannot
distinguish his ingredients from mine. But this is not an appropriate moment for theological disputation. I am dying because
I am unemployed. The bourgeoisie casts me off and the proletariat—the proletariat does not want to believe in my existence
in spite of concrete proof and considers me a creation of the
bourgeoisie. But you, by what right did you interfere in the execution of an action that is so difficult to repeat?"

"Never mind about that. I am just repaying an old debt. I
am one of those you stopped from suicide with a similar gesture,
appearing unexpectedly, miraculously, and fantastically. I am
repaying a debt of gratitude. I do not believe that you who are
so endowed with talent and experience need to commit suicide
because of unemployment. I believe that we can find even you
an occupation. I've got it!" he said after a moment's silence. "You
have been a viewer of the history of humanity from its inception.
Finding yourself at a certain distance, however, you saw it but

didn't hear it. Or, to put it another way: you were the viewer of a photographic history of the world, a viewer of a historical film. That being the case, it is impossible that you should not have acquired certain photogenic qualities. I am certain that you would make a first-rate film artist. Film is a great thing. Film gives you unmatched popularity. Finally, film is the first universal theater of the imagination in centuries, and a place where it will be easy to make contact with humanity. I see you more clearly now: the spirit of restlessness, the spirit of anarchy—you will fight with order, with organization, with the machine. You will be their battle, their embrace, their tragic dissonance, melancholy, their buffoon, their dance. You will be an anarchist dancing with a machine—an ingenious metaphor for the present day. You will be a hundred-story slaughterhouse from Chicago, filled with the refinements of a dozen Louvres. You will be the Eiffel Tower of the spirit, advertising Citröens. The eternal nihilist and corrupter, your face will express sadness and despair, metaphysics and goodness, the depth of cosmic melancholy, the soul, soul of humanity, which is your true essence. O Lucifer! your hands will be America, a machine, Taylorism,* a biomechanic. And the discrepancy between the tragic soul of your face and your mechanized movements will show people their caricature. A consistent anarchist, you will negate not just laws but things. A watch brought to a pawnshop, for example, will be treated like a patient. You will check its reflexes and pump it full of gas like a car. On the screen you will treat the watch the way you treated the great watch of the world. For you are sufficiently wise to understand that humanity demands anarchy to the end.

"And so your wish since the beginning of time will be granted—for, by negating things, you will become equal to God who created them in an act of affirmation."

The stranger vanished just as miraculously, unexpectedly, and fantastically as he had appeared.

Lucifer looked at the revolver that lay next to him on the marble tabletop.

*Method of factory management first developed and advocated by Frederick W. Taylor.—TRANS.

"Oh, well," he muttered to himself, "it would not have done any good anyway. I forgot I am immortal."

He returned the revolver to his pocket, paid his bill and left. The day—a foggy, autumn day—was well underway. Throngs of workers hurried like so many gray clouds to the factories. Newspaper vendors shouted the short names of the city's morning prayers.

Lucifer became a film artist.

We all know him.

He's Charlie Chaplin.